LUCKY 13

Tales from the John Radcliffe Bus

Edited by
Janet Bolam

BOMBUS BOOKS
15 Henleys Lane, Drayton, OX14 4HU
www.bombusbooks.co.uk
www.fast-print.net/store.php

Lucky 13
© Janet Bolam 2015

ISBN 978-178456-262-5

A catalogue record for this book is available from the British Library
Typeset by Anne Joshua, Oxford

First published 2015 by
BOMBUS BOOKS
an imprint of Fast-Print Publishing
Peterborough, England

Disclaimer
Lucky 13 is fiction. Although it is based on many well-known places
around Oxford any reference to living individuals is accidental.

Contents

Acknowledgements

This collection of short stories is based around Service 13 of the Oxford Bus Company and its authors would like to acknowledge the company's enthusiastic support for its publication. In particular, we would like to thank Andrew Morison for using the company's facilities in its promotion, Gwyn Smith for his technical advice and Marta Skorupinska for the cover design and graphics.

Similarly, the hospital charity, Oxford Radcliffe Hospitals Charitable Funds (registered charity 1057295) is using its resources to promote the book among the staff, patients and volunteers across the Trust's hospitals. All proceeds from the book's sale are being donated to the *Hidden Heroes Fund* which supports staff recognition, development and training. It is with great pleasure that both the Oxford Bus Company and Oxford Inc writers are collaborating to maximise its potential.

Jackie Vickers and Paul Bolam have assisted Janet Bolam on editorial matters and the publishing process has been co-ordinated by Andrew Bax.

Oxford Inc

Andrew Bax was once a publisher and now spends part of his time writing short stories and biographies. He is also involved with the John Radcliffe Hospital and often takes the No 13 bus to get there.

Graham Bird has been an enthusiastic fiction writer for the last ten years after a career in information technology. He enjoys psychological thrillers and crime novels, and loves to set his stories around Oxford, or on the coast of Cornwall where he was born.

Janet Bolam's birthday falls on May 13th. For dramatic effect, she sometimes tells people it was also a Friday, although it wasn't. She recommends the ploy as a great way to start a conversation with strangers.

Jenny Burrage attends three writers groups in Oxford. She leaves her car at home in Abingdon and always travels in on the X13. A wonderful service.

Heather Gelles Ebner lives in Oxford with her husband, two boys and a hamster. An expat from New York, she's learned to love the rain and queues but is still working on Marmite.

Neil Hancox has contributed to six or seven printed anthologies and three eBooks; a few years ago he won first prize in a Ramblers Holidays travel writing competition. He regularly journeys from Abingdon to Oxford and back on the X3 or X13 bus and sometimes takes the 13 to the JR.

Jackie Vickers has had many different and interesting occupations but now prefers to escape into imaginary worlds of her own making.

Annie Winner has always dabbled in life writing. Fiction is a new venture allowing her to indulge her hunch that you should never let truth get in the way of a good story.

Introduction

Janet Bolam

If we had a keen vision and feeling of all ordinary human life, it would be like hearing the grass grow, and the squirrels heart beat, and we should die of that roar which lies on the other side of silence.

George Eliot

For many of us, using a bus is a routine event, the way we travel from one place to another. We may know some of the faces we see, may even have made a friend or two who ride the same bus regularly, but for the most part, our fellow passengers are strangers.

This collection of short stories is about a particular bus journey that happened one Thursday in June 2015. The No 13 left Oxford Railway Station at 1.15 in the afternoon, and arrived 43 minutes later at the John Radcliffe Hospital. There was nothing special about this journey; the No 13 does the same route 49 times a day, Monday to Friday, passing 25 bus stops as it winds through the city centre, across the Plain to Marston, through the Northway Estate to Headington and the John Radcliffe Hospital (the JR as some locals call it). However, in each of these stories the lid is lifted on the lives of some of those passengers riding on the bus on that particular day, on that particular journey, revealing how extraordinary an ordinary bus journey can be, how, behind the polite façade, there lie hopes, passions, joy, heartache, sorrows and secrets.

A nurse, on his way to work, finds something on the bus that changes his life, Frances steels herself to make the journey she dreads, Mrs Hemmingway and Mrs Riley exchange their weekly gossip, Harold nurses his dark secret, and what's so important about the bag clutched anxiously by an elderly, well-dressed woman?

These stories have been written by Oxford Inc, a group of Oxford-based writers.

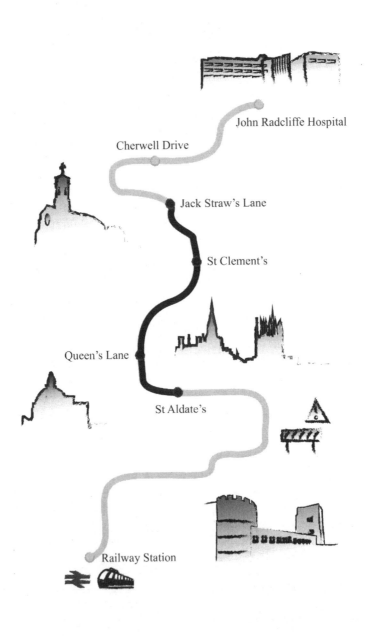

John Radcliffe Hospital

Cherwell Drive

Jack Straw's Lane

St Clement's

Queen's Lane

St Aldate's

Railway Station

Roast Potatoes

Andrew Bax

Harold had a feeling that this was going to be an important day so he chose one of the silk ties that Mrs Herbert gave him when her husband passed away, polished his shoes and wore his best cap. But just as he was ready to leave, he couldn't find his bus pass. The thought of paying £3.50 for his return fare made him so irritable that he nearly rang the solicitor to say he wasn't coming. So even though this was going to be an important day, he set off for the city centre feeling rather out of sorts.

Now, his business done, he was waiting in St Aldate's for the bus back to Marston. It was a sunny day and, yes – he had to admit it – his meeting had turned out rather well. So well in fact, that he had nearly bought a copy of the *Big Issue* from the man by the Post Office. When the bus arrived he settled himself in a seat towards the front, just across the aisle from a couple of peculiar-looking women. The younger of the two had dyed her hair a vivid red, the other's was white but whether from age or from a bottle, Harold couldn't tell. Tattoos and metal fixings too, he shouldn't wonder. Ageing punks, he decided, both of them. They seemed to be having a bit of a barney.

His meetings with the solicitor – and he'd had a few over the years – usually turned out satisfactorily. There was talk of tax exemptions, trusts and leases and although Harold didn't understand a word of it, it seemed to be all right. Just as well really, after all the uncertainty about his domestic arrangements. Harold didn't like uncertainty and the last few weeks had been rather unsettling.

Ever since Betty died, his neighbour Mrs Herbert had taken it upon herself to clean Harold's house and do his ironing. Not to be outdone, Mrs Vincent, his neighbour on the other side, made him a stew on Mondays and a roast dinner on Thursdays. All three of them had outlived their partners and were of an age to appreciate routine but a few weeks ago, Mrs Herbert had suddenly announced her intention of moving to Lowestoft to live with her sister.

The repercussions hit Harold hard. Never in his life had he done any housework and without the rivalry between Mrs Herbert and Mrs Vincent, he feared his stews and roast dinners could be in jeopardy.

But he was in luck. A few days later an outraged Mrs Herbert burst in on him to announce that her sister had taken in a man to live with her. A man, moreover, who was half her age and still married. She had met him at the Wednesday afternoon tea dances on the pier. There would be no room for Mrs Herbert. She was clearly upset and, to give him his due, Harold was properly sympathetic. However, there was no longer any need for him to think about paying someone to do his housework or to worry about the stews and roast dinners. For Harold, who was careful with his money, the news came as a great relief.

He was brought back to the present by a sharp exchange between the women across the aisle. The younger one seemed to be crying. Harold rather regretted not buying the *Big Issue* because he could pretend to be reading it while peering over the top. But there was no need to pretend anything because they were shouting now, with expletives. Harold didn't like strong language in a woman, although Mrs Herbert swore sometimes. He didn't much like it in men either. He never swore himself.

Suddenly, the older woman got up and plonked herself next to him. If Harold thought he would now have a ring-side seat, he was disappointed. This was clearly the interval between rounds. But as far as he could make out, the younger one had thrown out her man because he had taken up with another woman and, without his wages, she couldn't afford anywhere to live. And on top of that, her daughter was saddled with a couple of kids. Probably on benefits, Harold sniffed. He had no time for that kind of loose-living and neither, by the sound of it, had the woman sitting next to him. Although now sitting in grim-faced silence, she had made her opinions clear enough to the whole bus. Good for her.

But Harold had more important things to think about and decided that, when he got home, he would potter about on his allotment to unwind. It was his allotment that showed Harold's generous side. He gave nearly all its produce to Mrs Herbert and Mrs Vincent. They had been getting broad beans and lettuces for a week or two, the runners were coming on nicely and soon there would be courgettes and tomatoes. When the glut came, as it always did, he was able to offload armfuls of vegetables to them. What they did with such abundance is unknown, but they always seemed grateful. At Christmas he also gave a bottle of sherry to Mrs Herbert, who liked a drink, and a tin of Quality Street to Mrs Vincent.

For someone like Harold, saving had always come naturally, ever since he received his first wage packet. As an apprentice fitter at the works he never went out with the rest of the lads. He didn't follow Oxford United and didn't go to the cinema much. Instead he took up fishing and spent most of his weekends under a large green umbrella on the river-bank above Iffley Lock. If the truth be told, Harold was a bit of a loner.

What Betty had seen in him was anyone's guess. She was a good, wholesome girl; rather large and not the brightest perhaps, but that didn't matter. In any event, it was clear that Betty doted on him and seemed perfectly content with the simple life that she and Harold shared together for nearly 50 years. Once they were married, they rented a little terraced house at the top of William Street and never moved. To begin with, Betty sometimes wondered about babies, but they never talked about that sort of thing, and nothing happened. It had been an uneventful marriage and succeeded because neither partner made demands upon the other. When it came to money-matters, Betty naturally left everything to Harold because he was so careful.

However, a few years into their marriage, Harold seemed to be having a funny turn. He couldn't sleep, he lost his appetite and became withdrawn. Betty persuaded him to go to the doctor and whatever it was he prescribed seemed to do the trick. Suddenly Harold slept and ate better, and was clearly a lot happier. But, unknown to Betty, he hadn't been to the doctor. Instead he had been to a solicitor whose wise advice had lifted the burden of anxiety that afflicted him. Harold had suddenly become wealthy.

How it happened was really quite simple. Ernie had picked his number in the Premium Bonds, the big one. Some men may have shared this information with their wives, but not Harold. Betty did not understand money and so much of it would only worry her; besides, he had left everything to her in his will so she could do what she liked with it when he was gone. The thought that she might go first had never occurred to him.

The solicitor had advised Harold to try to buy his house from the landlord so that he could save on rent, and offered to make enquiries on his behalf. It so happened that the landlord was having a spot of bother with the tax man and was only too glad to enter into negotiations. While Betty thought Harold was still under the doctor he was, in fact, under the solicitor. The upshot was that he didn't just buy his house, he bought quite a chunk of William Street. The solicitor set him up as sole proprietor of a company called Leicester Land Management, 'just in case' (Harold didn't understand why but the notion appealed to his cautious nature). The business was managed by a letting agency which paid all the rental income into a savings account in Jersey, and life returned to normal.

For some months afterwards Harold considered telling Betty about their good fortune but he didn't know how to go about it; she would only tell the neighbours and that would never do. The passage of time offered no solution to this dilemma and the longer he put off telling her, the more difficult it seemed to become. Harold was one of those people who thought that if you ignored a problem for long enough, it would simply go away. So that is exactly what he did.

Then, some 40 years later, Betty had her stroke. It is often the case that one only realises how much one depends on someone when they are gone. That was how it was with Harold. He couldn't even boil an egg. So Mrs Herbert and Mrs Vincent took him in hand. It is difficult for a single man to struggle on a pension, they reasoned, particularly now that Leicester Land Management had just put up all their rents.

But a few weeks ago Harold had received a letter, addressed to the Managing Director of Leicester Land Management, from agents acting of behalf of clients seeking 'development land'. Harold had never thought of himself as a Managing Director before and although he quite liked the title, it implied an unwelcome measure of responsibility. So, despite the letter's reference to 'matters to our mutual advantage' and 'confidential discussion', he put it in a drawer.

Now the agents had written again, revealing this time that their client was Oxford Brookes University. They wanted to build more student flats and if Harold would agree to sell them a bit of William Street he would be enriched by 'a very substantial sum'. The prospect of adding to the considerable fund that had accumulated in Jersey had obvious appeal, but it had its difficulties too. Of those, the main one was that he, and most of his neighbours in William Street, would have to find somewhere else to live. Another was that he might be revealed as the owner of Leicester Land Management. But most of all, he worried about life without Mrs Vincent's roast potatoes. Marvellous, they were, crisp and golden on the outside, soft and crumbly on the inside.

It was a problem that Harold couldn't resolve, which is why he had again been to the solicitor, the same one who had been so helpful in the past. When they first met he had been a trainee but now he was a senior partner, and he had got to know Harold's way of thinking. Harold explained the problem and showed him the plans. The solicitor studied them for a while, took some measurements with a ruler, made a few sketches and calculations on a piece of paper, grunted and reached a conclusion. It seemed to him that if Brookes would agree to a small change in the plans, most of the demolition would be on the other side of the road and the houses occupied by Harold, Mrs Herbert and Mrs Vincent would be spared. He also assured him that no-one need know about the ownership of Leicester Land Management. He then offered to contact the agents with the proposal and obtain a valuation for the property. Something in excess of £2 million, he thought. Would that be acceptable? Harold said yes.

The bus turned into Marston Road and soon they were

approaching Harold's stop. It had been a good meeting and he was feeling pretty chuffed with himself. His cleaning, ironing, stews and roast dinners were still safe. Plus, he would have a bit more money in the bank. And another plus, that toffee-nosed college man across the road was going to have his house demolished. But just as he was waiting to get off, Harold felt something in his pocket. He couldn't believe it, but there it was, his bus pass. His first thought was to negotiate a refund from the driver but, feeling the gaze of the other passengers behind him, he decided against it. He could, he supposed, afford £3.50 and consoled himself with the thought that in just a few hours he would be eating Mrs Vincent's roast potatoes.

John Radcliffe Hospital

Cherwell Drive

Jack Straw's Lane

St Clement's

Queen's Lane

St Aldate's

Railway Station

A Perfect Ending

JACKIE VICKERS

Judith is surprised that it takes so long to get to the hospital. The roads are congested with heavy traffic, constantly held up by road works, but perhaps it is always like this in Oxford. Although she was brought up in this city, it is many years since she went anywhere by bus, for her mother lives near the railway station and Judith's visits are as brief and infrequent as possible. This suits them both as, for some years now, her mother spends most of her time writing and promoting her books. Annabel Leigh is a successful writer of popular historical crime fiction, which Judith, preferring fact to fiction, finds unreadable.

The bus driver makes an emergency stop, sending his passengers crashing into the seats in front. They bump their knees, drop parcels and there is loud swearing from the back of the bus. Judith peels the wrapper from her third chocolate bar this morning. She craves sweet things continuously when she is visiting her mother. The bus lurches as it accelerates again and the chocolate paper falls to the floor. As she bends to retrieve it she sees the woman across the gangway is reading an Annabel Leigh bodice-ripping murder mystery. They are published in lurid magenta covers, which Judith knows well, for signed copies of the latest in the series arrive regularly at her flat.

'Write a nice review for me, darling.'

'I'm a Medical Correspondent,' Judith protests each time. 'Not my thing.'

'Oh? Surely journalists can turn their hands to anything. And it might be useful to have something else to fall back on – should anything happen.'

'Happen?'

'Well, yours is not a very secure job, is it?'

Judith wants say that being on the staff of a reputable daily paper has more security than being a freelance writer, but knows better than to argue with her mother. As the bus moves slowly past the striking facades of college buildings, Judith wonders how her mother had felt on her arrival, nearly 50 years ago, as the newly married wife of a rising star in the university History Department. Unfortunately as the years passed, her father's reputation dwindled. For Florian Leigh, though charismatic and charming, had lacked ambition. Twenty years after his death, who now remembers the handful of scholarly papers on the changing status of Hampshire shepherds 1350–1390? Or the book that took the history world by storm: *Medieval Farming Practices in the Test Valley*? For these once ground-breaking publications were never followed up and his students, many of whom had turned to history merely to sit at his feet, lost interest. Some said he was quite simply lazy, for he neither announced plans for further research, nor was he ever seen near a library.

Florian's usual response to his wife's bitter recriminations regarding the eclipse of his once glittering career, had been to raise his glass of expensive red wine in a gesture of self-mockery. For Florian Leigh had made no attempt to please either his wife or his colleagues but gradually detached himself from as much of academic life as he could get away with. He had only ever told one person of the sudden awakening he had experienced while walking up Catte Street, one warm evening in June. A beam of light had cast a warm glow over the Radcliffe Camera, and it struck him, as he stopped to admire the architecture, that he no longer had any interest in the contents of that remarkable building. He thought of all those books, which had so excited him on his arrival, and now wondered that they should mean so little to him. How much of this change of heart lay in his growing attachment to the young woman he spent his afternoons with is hard to say. In appearance she was pleasant but unremarkable. She laughed at his jokes, was discreet, and made no demands. For the first time in his life, Florian had the love and uncritical support of a woman who had no interest in furthering his career, nor in the trappings of academic life. Relieved that nothing was now expected of him, he felt free to delight in the ordinariness of his new existence. No-one, least of all Annabel, knew of her husband's parallel life until he unexpectedly took early retirement, while Judith was still at school, and slipped away to a quiet life in a remote Oxfordshire village.

For some months a shocked Annabel retreated into herself. She told her daughter some story about her father needing time and space to recover his health. By the time Judith left for university, Florian's departure was no longer of any interest to the gossips. Annabel eventually emerged furious but determined to retrieve something notable from the ruins of her marriage and began work to turn a personal disaster into a public triumph. The detective and hero of her historical series, Sir Roland Mortimer, heir to estates in Kent and Northumberland, was none other than a taller, wealthier version of Florian Leigh. True to the traditions of aristocratic detectives, his foppish ways concealed acute observation and sharp intelligence and closely resembled the man her husband had become with his lazy charm and roving eye. Annabel had made the eighteenth century her own, untroubled by historical accuracy nor by the smirks and gossip of her husband's former colleagues and she had steadily risen to command a high place on the best-sellers' list. Florian, on the page, gave Annabel status and a devoted following, furthermore, she has become a very rich woman. Judith, who finds the books repetitive, lacking in depth and emotionally superficial, tries for the sake of harmony to conceal her distaste. After all, thousands of enthusiastic readers hold a different view.

The bus shudders as it comes to a stop. Judith steps down into the warm sunshine and walks briskly towards the entrance. Though she frequently visits hospitals, research establishments and other large facilities, today she is finding the layout of the John Radcliffe Hospital difficult to negotiate. She feels confused, and even disorientated as she struggles to find her way. Her mother's admission to hospital has shaken and destabilised her more than she could have expected. There have been many mutual disagreements over the years and even occasions of active dislike, but this sick woman is, after all, her closest living relative. Eventually she asks for the Cardiac Unit and feels foolish as the nurse points to the sign above her head. Another corridor, more double doors and at last she can see her mother's bed. A nurse emerges from the bay and draws back the curtains and there is Annabel, bent over her handbag, searching for something. A little pale perhaps, and drawn about the eyes.

'Darling! At last!' Annabel holds her hands up and turns her head away, kissing the air. Judith settles herself on a chair by the bed, feeling relief at her mother's relatively normal appearance.

'Nothing to worry about. I'm only here under observation. They'll do more tests tomorrow and then you can take me home.'

Annabel examines her hands and begins to file her nails. Judith, who has spent her working life writing about medical matters, presses for more details, then realises that her mother's confident words cannot be borne out by the evidence. On reflection, she can see that Annabel would hardly be taking up a bed otherwise.

'I can ill afford time in hospital,' her mother continues, 'my publishers are waiting for the last few chapters.'

She says this in a loud voice and looks around for any reaction, but her fellow patients are either asleep or are wearing headphones.

Later, Judith looks round the ward while her mother rests. There is plenty to see: nurses hook patients up to equipment, push laden trolleys here and there and speak to the many visitors. Now a bed is being pushed into place in the adjoining bay and the curtains are drawn. Voices are low and reassuring as nurses come and go. Then other staff come for Annabel and take her away for some procedure. Eventually the curtains round the next bed are drawn back and Judith finds herself face-to-face with an elderly grey-faced woman who is propped up on several pillows and appears to have trouble breathing.

The woman nods at the vacant space. 'It seems I have a famous neighbour.' Judith fidgets. She never knows what to say when her mother's writing is mentioned.

'Do you read historical fiction?'

'Not really. Years ago I worked in a small gift shop: cards, china ornaments, that sort of thing. We kept a good stock of popular novels, and your mother's books were always in demand. I take it she is your mother?'

Judith nods. She has always found it difficult to speak to strangers, especially in hospitals. Some people can chat about anything, the weather or parking spaces, even health. It seems impertinent to enquire about a person's illness. Though Judith makes a living from writing on medical topics, she prefers considering health issues in the abstract, feeling more comfortable with statistics, research papers and clinical trials. Chatting seems to come easily to this elderly woman, however, whose only problem is her breathing. Her bright eyes examine Judith without blinking. She looks rather like a mouse.

'It can't have been easy growing up with a famous writer.' The mousy woman speaks slowly and so quietly that Judith has to move nearer to hear.

'She wasn't well-known until after I left home.'

'Did you feel under pressure to write yourself? Having parents in the business, as it were.'

These questions seem rather personal. She would not herself ask this sort of thing and does not feel obliged to reply and picks up a magazine from her mother's locker. She turns a few pages and looks up to see the woman staring at her.

'Did it trouble you much when your father left? There's a lot of biographical information to be gleaned from book covers,' she explains, raising her eyebrows.

Judith catches her breath. She is unused to such a direct question. During the first months after Florian's departure no-one mentioned him. It was like a death in the family without mourners or flowers or condolences. Especially not condolences. There was just a terrible void. Her mother was tight-lipped and silent and friends, teachers, neighbours, skirted round the subject. Judith feels hot and uncomfortable. Was this information really on the loose covers of Annabel's books? She had never noticed. She gets up without answering and walks slowly towards a desk where nurses stand, clustered around a computer. One of them turns towards her with a smile.

'Can you tell me when my mother is expected back? Only I want to be here when she returns.'

Judith remembers passing a newsagent and a café. There should be plenty of time to read a paper while she drinks her coffee which she hopes will put the mousy woman's nosy questions out of her mind. She recalls her mother's complaints about her fans, many years ago.

'They come to Literary Festivals and Book Launches but are more interested in what you had for breakfast than about your writing,' she had said, lighting another cigarette. Judith remembers her unsympathetic reply.

'Well, they do buy your books!'

'They would rather buy a piece of *me*.' She scattered ash everywhere as she waved her hand.

Judith can understand better now. She thinks it must be one of the worst things to be trapped in a hospital bed next to someone you would normally do anything to avoid. And for her mother this would naturally be some gushing fan. She sips her coffee, which is extraordinarily good, and opens her paper, but the mousy woman's words keep coming back to her as if on a loop. And then it occurs to her that a gift shop, which might well have a shelf full of historical novels, would never try to sell academic books or journals. How then would she know about Florian's book? Could she have worked in one of the college libraries, an ageing spinster in awe of academic achievement? As she lies in a hospital bed, her sparse grey hair pulled back into a bun and struggling to breathe, there is little indication of what she might have looked like in her prime. Judith gets up suddenly, grabs her bag and, letting her paper fall to the floor, hurries back to the ward. She feels compelled, without knowing why, to protect her mother from her neighbour, inoffensive though she might appear. Then, as she approaches the ward she hears an alarm, followed by people rushing.

Nurses and doctors come running, someone is pushing some equipment towards the elderly woman's bed. The other patients all turn to look, but the curtains are swiftly drawn and there is nothing to see. Judith has witnessed all the turmoil from the doorway and is relieved to see that her mother is leaning back on her pillow seemingly unaffected, or certainly uninterested, by the drama around her. As she approaches she hears her mother humming. Then the curtains are drawn back and as the bed is wheeled away, Judith sees that a mask has been placed over the mousy woman's face.

'I wonder where they're taking her,' Annabel says languidly. 'Intensive care? Surgery?' she pauses, 'The morgue?'

Judith looks at her. Annabel waves her scarlet-tipped fingers at the vacant space.

'I used to wish she would die,' she says, and leans over to take her handbag from her locker. She finds a mirror and begins to apply lipstick. 'Of course that was before she began to go to seed,' she explains through stretched lips which she slowly coats with a bright magenta.

'So she was . . .'

Annabel nods and replaces the mirror. 'She didn't know that I knew. Until now.'

'What did you say to her?'

But Annabel seems not to hear. She is looking up at the ceiling, a slow smile creeping over her face.

'The perfect ending,' she whispers. 'Pass me my notebook, Judith.'

The Gift

Janet Bolam

It was late morning when I threw myself into a low chair in the nurses' office on ward 7A. Don, the senior nurse and a good mate, was juggling phones and paperwork. He thrust a tub of Quality Street in my direction with seemly gravity.

'There's only the strawberry creams left,' I observed wryly. 'Nothing's going right. I could be watching Loose Women with my feet up.'

'I grant you that, but then you'd miss all the fun. How's it going out there?'

'Down in admissions? No beds. A&E jammed with trolleys.'

'And your day is just about to get better. You need to witness a change to a will and we have to do it this afternoon.' Don flicked through a folder of nursing notes.

'Why does it have to be me?'

'Because the nursing staff are too busy and it's what duty managers do.'

'That's a new one on me.'

'The patient's name is Countess Irina Alexandrovich.'

'Royalty?'

'Russian royalty. It doesn't count. She's 81 years old, admitted early this morning with a gastrointestinal bleed – normally under Harry Markham.'

'The gastro surgeon?'

'That's him.'

'Handsome'

'Stop it!'

'So you want me to get her moved to a surgical ward?'

'She's actually his private patient.'

'Before you say another word, no beds in the Private Wing either.'

'You're kidding.'

'Unfortunately, I'm not.'

'OK. Here's the thing. She's refusing treatment and for the time being, she's refusing pain relief.'

'How awful.'

'I think she's just had enough. She's been fighting bowel cancer for years and there's nothing we can do now, except help her with pain, and deal with episodes like this. Unless the bleeding stops of its own accord and quite soon, her chances of getting through the day are slim.'

'And she's changing her will? Wow. So what do I have to do?'

'We have protocols. We have to establish that she's of sound disclosing mind.'

'You mean check she's not doolally?'

'I'm loving the sensitivity Ruth! Yes. We have to satisfy ourselves that she knows what she's doing and that the consequences are clear to her. I've left a message for Harry to come up as soon as he's finished in theatre. He'll have to assess her.'

'Bleep me when you need me and I'll come straight up.' I rose wearily, collecting a strawberry cream on my way. It was better than nothing.

Klara stepped off the train and wondered where all the porters were. She had left her small valise in the first class carriage and she needed one to help her from the train and into a taxi to the hospital. Abdul just happened to be passing on his way to a much-needed tea break. He tried to explain that there were no porters anymore, but she wasn't listening. Amused, he collected her valise and steered her out of the station.

'Could you summon a taxi for me?' she requested from on-high. There were none to be seen and a huge queue was forming at the taxi rank. Klara did not intend to be left waiting in a queue.

'What can you do for me?' she held out a £20 note. 'I need to get to the hospital as a matter of urgency.' Abdul was now uncomfortable. This wasn't his job, the clock was ticking on his tea break, and he certainly wasn't accepting any money from this condescending lady.

'You'll have to join the queue I'm afraid.'

'But I have to get to the hospital as a matter of urgency!' she repeated.

The bus to the JR was about to set off as Abdul climbed aboard and parked her valise on a seat near the front. He tipped his cap as he imagined porters might do, handed the £20 note to the bus driver with a wink, and left her to it.

The bus swung out of the Station. Klara couldn't take it in. On a bus. She was on a bus. She had never been on one before and now she felt imprisoned by it. She had to stay on it all the way to the hospital because if she got off, who knows what would happen? What sort of a place had no taxis? With a slight panic she arranged herself so her valise was on one seat and herself on the other; there was no way anyone was going to sit next to her. With a wave of irritation, she cursed her brother. Why was he in California just when she needed him? If he had been around, the hospital would have called him, not her. As things were, it was she who had to dash to the hospital to tend to her estranged mother.

The bus stopped. A small woman, mid phone conversation, had stepped onto the bus, but was now standing stock still as if frozen to the spot, preventing anyone else getting on or off. There was some sort of scrap with the person standing behind her, and eventually, the bus driver intervened and she literally tottered off the bus and back onto the pavement. Klara concluded she must be drunk and clutched her valise even closer.

Klara found her mother propped up in bed, wide-awake.

'I've just been talking to the nurses.'

'What about "hello mother, how are you? I'm sorry you're in hospital"?' her mother responded.

'Of course I'm sorry you're in hospital. I came straight away. How are you?'

'I'm fine. What do *you* think?'

'The nurse told me something that can't be true.'

'It is true.'

'You don't know what I'm going to say yet.'

'Oh yes I do, and yes, it's true. I don't want any more treatment.'

Klara found a chair, dropped her coat and hat onto it, and sighed with frustration.

'I'm not listening to this nonsense, Mother. You need treatment to stop the bleeding and then you'll be fine.'

'I've made my decision.'

'If Pieter was here, you wouldn't be pulling this silly trick.' Klara looked around her mother's hospital bed, the curtains drawn around it.

'I've had enough.'

But Klara wasn't listening.

'We need to get you moved to the private ward and I'll bring you some nice flowers. This is horrible.'

'Don't start feeling guilty now, Klara. It's too late. And I'm serious.'

'Mother, if you don't agree to be treated, you'll die. You know that don't you?'

'Yes.'

'You want to die?' In the bald silence that followed, Klara sank onto her mother's bed.

'So they'll save me this time. But what for? More chemotherapy? More surgery? This way I'll never be a burden to you.'

'Whoever said you'd be a burden?'

'Oh, so I'd come and live with you would I? You and your lovely boyfriend Sergei?'

'Stephan, actually. Are you doing this to punish me?'

'No, I'm not punishing you, I'm saving you,'

'It's time you stopped trying to save me.' Klara returned bitterly. Her mother's face screwed up with pain. Klara leapt to her feet.

'Are you all right? Shall I help you to lie down properly? What can I do?'

'No, no, it'll pass. Just help me move up the bed.'

Klara couldn't remember when she and her mother had last had any sort of physical contact, and she wasn't prepared for the visceral wave of sorrow and regret that overwhelmed her as she carefully slid her mother's frail body into a sitting position.

'Mother, I beg you, let them treat you. Please.'

Her mother seemed not to hear.

'I have something to tell you.' She smoothed her hands on the sheet. There was no warmth in her voice and no eye contact. Klara's heart sank; the moment of intimacy had passed.

'You won't like it, but I've decided to change my will. I've decided not to leave you the tiara.'

'I'm sorry, I don't understand.'

'I think you do.'

'You don't want me to have the tiara?' gasped Klara.

'I think that would be best.' her mother continued, a slight tremor in her voice.

'You could have changed your will years ago. Why now?'

'I've decided to leave it to the Hermitage in St Petersburg,' her mother continued.

'It's my birthright,' whispered Klara.

'The museum will care for it, as it should be.'

'I'd care for it, just like you did, just like your mother did. Why are you doing this?'

'I've asked for my solicitor to come this afternoon.'

'You haven't answered my question!'

'Do you really want me to?'

'As a matter of fact, yes I do.'

'When did you last phone me or visit? When did you last ask how I was, or – or do anything a daughter ought to do? When did you last behave as a daughter should?'

Klara looked at her mother, her cold blue eyes dull with drugs and pain, and tried not to bite back.

'Why don't you sleep on it. Decide what to do tomorrow, when Pieter's here.'

'Don't be so stupid Klara. I might not be here tomorrow.'

Klara walked to the window and tried to gather her thoughts, but it wasn't a time to be rational. She turned like a wounded animal.

'I don't understand what I've ever done to you to make you be so cruel. It's the last thing you'll ever do, and it's this? I want to remember you with kindness, not like this! Not this.'

Klara only knew she was shouting when a nurse came to take her away.

'We've had a right old time with the Countess.' Don briefed me early that afternoon. 'Her daughter arrived this morning, up from London. A right piece of work. As soon as they laid eyes on each other, they were at each other's throats. We've had to keep them apart most of the day, which hasn't been easy and to be honest, we've got 25 other patients on the ward who need us too. Can you do me a favour? Have you got time to sit with the Countess? The solicitor'll be here very soon. Oh, and keep that daughter away from her?'

Countess Irina Alexandrovich was deathly pale, but a vision of dignity, her long grey hair gently caught into a bun, her face, noble and calm. As I stepped through the curtains that were drawn around her bed, the hum of the ward seemed to fall away. It was almost like a confessional. I had no idea what to say, so I just introduced myself and told her I was going to wait with her until the solicitor arrived and then I explained that I would be a witness.

'I'm so sorry our family difficulties have caused problems, and you've been thrown right into the middle of them. I'm afraid my daughter is quite volatile at times.' The Countess was clearly in pain but bearing it with a fierce dignity.

'Would you like me to call a nurse?'

'No, they'll only want to give me drugs. I want to have all my wits about me when the solicitor comes. But can you help me lie down? I find it hard to be comfortable.'

She'd just dozed off when I heard the sharp beating of stiletto on lino crack through the ward. It was the daughter making her way towards her mother's bed with grim determination. She was a force to behold. Long, dark, carefully coiffured red hair, blood-red fingernails and sharply tailored suit, she was a woman who expected to get her own way.

'I'm sorry, but for the moment, the senior nurse has asked that she's not disturbed.' I was surprised at how assertive I was being.

'Who are you?' Klara demanded.

'I'm the Duty Manager. Perhaps you could wait in the day room? Have you been offered a cup of tea?'

'Tea? No thank you.' Her accent was cut glass. 'I understand my mother will be able to go to the Private Wing in the morning, but in the meantime I want her moved to a single room.'

'She's in the observation bay so the nurses can keep a close eye on her. It's the best place she can be.'

'Are you clinically qualified?' She leaned forward, and eyed my hospital badge. 'Ruth Slater, Patient Services Manager, please, tell me, in what world does a hospital manager have authority to prevent me from seeing my mother? We weren't in a communist state last time I looked, and you, Ruth Slater, are in no position to get in my way.'

Fortunately Don intervened and suggested that they try to contact the consultant to see if she could talk to him, and with his hand gently on her arm, they retreated to his office.

'Was that Klara?' murmured the Countess when I returned to her bedside. 'Her bark's worse than her bite, but I fear you may experience a lot more bite in the near future.' The Countess seemed revived by her short nap.

'You know,' she began quietly, 'I have a tiara, given to my mother by the last Tsar. It's set with diamonds and emeralds. Priceless because its provenance is unimpeachable. You know, before the revolution, the balls held at the palace were very special. They all wore tiaras of course, but not many wore one given by the Tsar himself. I have a photograph of my mother posing with members of the Russian royal family and she's wearing it then. 1915. When my Mother was young, she was bewitching. Some say I was the Tsar's daughter. Nonsense of course.' She gave a careless, almost flirtatious wave of her hand as she lapsed into silence. Then, from nowhere, her mood darkened.

'I did something I can never tell anyone, not even a priest.' She gave a dry cough, her hands whipping to her stomach. Alarmed, I helped her to a small sip of water and suspected her mind was wandering. 'Many years ago, my daughter had a child,' she continued. 'The baby was deformed, a vegetable. When it was one day old, I took a pillow and smothered it.' The silence that followed was like the stillness after a loud gunshot. I held my breath. 'I did it for my daughter, so she could have a life. And the baby? The baby had no life to live. It was the hardest thing I ever did, but I will meet God with a clear conscience.' She coughed again, but waved the proffered cup of water away. 'My daughter and I have never spoken about it.'

'Would you like to?'

'Absolutely not,' she replied.

I could see that the Countess had become agitated and I did consider calling a nurse, but I found I was unable to move.

'My daughter and I clash. She tells me nothing about her life, and I tell her nothing about mine. With my son things are very different. He lives in California half the time. Makes films. You may have heard of him? Pieter Alexandovich?' Her face creased with a warm smile. 'He comes to see me whenever he can, always at the end of a phone, especially since I've been ill. Her? As far as she's concerned, I might as well be dead. Why should I leave the tiara to her? She only cares about herself.' A nurse whipped the curtains open and gave us both a start.

'The solicitor's here. He's in Don's office.'

Klara was as a ship in full sail. Don looked like he would prefer to hide behind his desk and Mr Chan, the solicitor, clutched his briefcase as if his life depended on it.

'My mother is mentally unstable. I don't care how many tests they, or you do to "satisfy yourselves" Mr. Chan. I'm her daughter and I know she would never, NEVER choose to die or to change her will. The whole thing is ludicrous.'

'It might be wise to speak to the doctor who assessed her,' returned Mr. Chan.

'I've been trying, but he's not answering,' Don sighed.

'Given how ill she is, I think we have no grounds for delay. I'm sorry if you find it uncomfortable Madam, but with respect, you aren't named as the next of kin,' said Mr. Chan.

'I'm her daughter, named next of kin or not, and if my brother were here, he would be behind me all the way. I demand a second opinion.'

'We've already done that and both of the consultants agree, she's of sound disclosing mind; she understands what she's doing,' said Don gently as Mr. Chan scanned the medical notes, 'and I'm concerned about any further delay. She's been refusing analgesics and she'll be in a lot of pain by now.'

'Then I'll go and see her right now. Miss Slater, I believe you are to act as witness? I think it would be best if it's just the two of us.'

The Countess was green with pain and unable to speak. I ran to get a nurse and very quickly, she was given the painkillers and sedation she needed and had fallen asleep. It was too late to change her will that night.

All that time spent on 7A meant I had a lot to do before I went home, and it was past 8 o'clock when I trudged past the café and saw Klara huddled in a corner. I was beyond tired, but I felt I had to go over to see how she was doing. Not good, it would seem. Her face was streaked with mascara and the virago I had met earlier in the day had transmuted into a small, sad wreck.

'I look such a mess,' she sniffed.

'It's been a hard day,' was all I could think of to say.

'You could say that. How's my mother?'

'We've moved her into a room of her own and she's asleep. You can go to her, and if you want to stay the night, that can be arranged.'

Klara nodded her thanks.

'She's going to be all right isn't she?'

'I'm not a doctor, I couldn't say,' I replied. Klara smiled in recognition of her earlier rudeness.

'You've been kind to my mother. Thank you. I know you had a long conversation with her. It should've been me there with her, but as you can see, it's difficult.'

I began to feel sorry for her.

'Would you mind telling me what you talked about?'

'I can't, I'm sorry.'

'But you know about the tiara?'

I nodded uncertain of the wisdom of any collusion.

'Did she tell you anything else?'

'I was with her quite a long time.'

'What else?' a wave of anxiety shaped her face.

'It's difficult,' I levelled, 'I have to respect patient confidentiality.'

She tried a withering look, but her fire had gone out and she just looked sad.

'You should make your peace with her.'

'Ruth Slater, there's no peace for me. My mother has done the most terrible thing and she has to talk to a priest. It doesn't matter what denomination, but she has to repent. Make her, I beg you, because I can't do it.'

'I'm not sure you can ask me to do that. It's her right to change her will.'

'I'm not talking about that!' snapped Klara. 'She told you, didn't she, about my baby?'

I was like a rabbit frozen in headlights; this conversation was spinning out of control and I wanted to get away.

'What did she tell you?' Klara leaned forward desperate.

'I shouldn't . . .'

'Tell me! Please.' I was not equipped to deal with the pain in her voice.

'She said she did it for you.' As the words tumbled out of my mouth, my brain was screeching 'Stop it! Don't say another word!'

'For me? For me? She murdered my baby for me?' Klara exclaimed. 'It was for her; it's always been about her. She never asked me what I thought or felt, she was too concerned to preserve the family name, her name.'

My mouth was dry. I said nothing.

'Find her a priest, Ruth Slater, find her a priest before it's too late.'

I nodded my consent. With an audible sigh of relief, Klara rose and placing a hand on my shoulder as she passed by, she paused. 'You are a better person than I ever could be.'

I watched her leave, and then as I promised, I collected the hospital Chaplain and together we climbed the stairs to the ward.

John Radcliffe Hospital

Cherwell Drive

Jack Straw's Lane

St Clement's

Queen's Lane

St Aldate's

Railway Station

Lucky 13

JENNY BURRAGE

Beverley Brown had not wanted to get up that morning. It hadn't been a good week. She wanted to turn over and forget all that had happened. Sometimes she stretched out in bed, trying to find Rick beside her, but his side was always empty.

Reaching fifty last Saturday had been like confronting a milestone. Half a century. Middle age. Amber was sorry not to be able to come home for her mother's birthday. Edinburgh University was a long way from Oxford and it was exam time for her daughter. Amber had sent flowers and Bev promised there would be a celebration when she came home at the end of June. She told her parents the same thing because they too were determined to visit. They knew she needed support. We shall all get together later, she promised them. Celebration? It would be hard but she would pretend for their sakes.

She was heading for the JR. Her next door neighbour, Bert, had fallen downstairs the previous evening. Luckily the old chap had been wearing one of those alarms round his neck and she was on first call. He looked grey and shaken and she had accompanied him to hospital in the ambulance. At A&E he was examined and although there were no bones broken, he seemed very dazed and they were keeping him in for more tests. Bev had promised to visit the next day and here she was on her way.

She parked in Osney Lane car park, the one she always used in Oxford when she was going shopping. She began her short walk to the station stepping her way in between the cones and road sign instructions to pedestrians. Road works were every-where these days. She hardly ever used buses but her friend advised her not to drive to the JR because of parking problems. Number 13 bus outside the station, she'd been told. They run frequently, very reliable. As she approached the R4 bus stop, she saw one leaving. She sighed and stood there looking about her.

She stared at the ochre spread of the Said Business School building opposite the bus stop which dominated the view, a well known part of the Oxford landscape now. She counted the layers in the pyramid roof-top. Twelve.

'Proper name is a ziggurat,' Rick had said. 'A stepped tower, the kind originally built in Mesopotamia.' He'd always told her things like that, little snippets of information which she remembered and loved. Loved him too. So much. She still couldn't believe he had left her a year ago. Seemed only like yesterday. They had even planned their silver wedding party at the Randolph. Now he was married to a woman half her age.

'You are middle-aged, ugly, overweight and boring, Beverley Brown,' said a voice inside her head. 'It's no wonder he left.'

She could feel the queue growing behind her. An open-topped tour bus stopped opposite. Maybe she could take one of her classes on a ride; she had discovered many of the children had little knowledge about the city. But it wasn't easy arranging trips when you were a supply teacher in a primary school. You never knew where you would be asked to go next. Fortunately she wasn't teaching this week so she was able to visit Bert.

The 13 rolled up and Bev paid and took a seat half way down the bus next to a smeary window. She rubbed her hand over the glass so she could see through it.

Just as the bus was about to leave, a man who was kitted out like a station employee got on waving what looked like a £20 note. He was followed by a smartly-suited woman. The driver appeared to fiddle about with some money but the man got off the bus without waiting for the change. The woman put her small travel bag down and sat next to it as if claiming the entire seat for herself. She ignored the driver. What a strange entrance to the bus, thought Bev. She looked important somehow.

Finally the bus moved off. How she missed her car and being in control of her journey. The bus rumbled and bumped into the city centre and Bev noticed the Alice Shop which

Amber had loved as a child, so did she herself of course. The Croissanterie bakery looked very inviting too. She hadn't had any lunch. Rick loved French cuisine. Rick. Rick. Rick. Always on her mind. Still in her world.

'I'm leaving you Bev. There's someone else.'

She had tried to scrub those words out of her mind but she couldn't. She had never suspected that he was having an affair. She had been happy but he obviously wanted more. He and his young secretary often travelled abroad as part of work. All those working late nights too. She trusted Rick and had brushed all other thoughts away. She had met his secretary once at a Christmas party and liked her. Then. A twenty-four year old statuesque blonde with a model figure had stolen her husband. My exact opposite she now realised. How naive she had been.

The bus moved over Magdalen Bridge on towards the Plain. Bev, Rick and Amber had been to a May morning event two years ago where they had mingled with the crowd, waiting for the choir to burst into song. Next came a huge breakfast in one of the many cafés which opened early. They did things together, always a threesome. Family outings like that were memorable. Gone now. She wondered how much Rick remembered. Probably too busy with his new life.

Amber refused to see or speak to her father and Bev was sad about that. Even though Amber was on her side, she felt it was important that she didn't lose touch with him. Everyone said she would come round eventually. There was a baby now as well and Amber had a half sister.

'Gross, Mum,' she had said when she heard the news.

So much had changed in both their lives. Sometimes Bev felt she couldn't go on. If it weren't for Amber . . .

Bev turned her attention to scenes outside the bus. Groups of back-packing tourists and school parties from abroad were gathering at the roadside. Excited faces. Chatter. Camera flashes. She wondered what they thought of Oxford. So much history to find. You saw more from the bus than you did when driving, she decided. The downside was too many bus stops. She liked fast travel.

She glanced round at her fellow passengers. They appeared

to be staring straight ahead like zombies. It was strange how people on buses rarely spoke to each other, she thought. Wasn't natural really, but she supposed they were as intent on getting to their destinations as she was.

At the next stop, near the Thai Orchid, a man got on. He paused for a moment, ignored any empty seats, and came and sat next to her.

'Mind if I open a window?' he asked.

'No. Please do.' It wasn't particularly warm. She felt his arm brush her coat as he stood up and leaned over her.

'Nice day, isn't it?' She saw cornflower-blue eyes and a strong mouth smiling. A rugged face with the hint of a beard looked down at her. She felt he was studying her. Younger than she was, maybe around forty.

'Yes.' The day was cloudy with a hint of sun, so yes it was nice she supposed.

'Going to the JR?' he asked.

'Yes.'

'Not ill are you?' She was surprised at this. He sounded concerned. Unusual from a complete stranger.

'No. Just visiting.'

'I'm not going there. I'm a gardener, working near there. Landscaping.'

'Oh.'

Bev could see his large hands were rough and his nails grubby. He was wearing cords and a worn denim jacket with the sleeves rolled up.

'I love trees,' he said suddenly.

'So do I.' She always had.

'Got a favourite tree?'

She considered this. 'Silver Birch, I think. So striking with their silvered bark.'

'Silvered,' he murmured, 'I like that. Clever. Never heard that before.'

'And you?'

'Oak. Big and strong.'

Like you, she thought.

'Do you like oaks as well?' he asked.

'Yes I do. They're majestic.'

'There you go again. You're good at words.'

'Am I?' For the first time that day Bev smiled. The bus stopped. Some passengers got off. The gardener-man looked at Bev. Was there more conversation coming she thought? There was. He seemed determined.

'I live on Cowley Road.'

'Oh.'

'Near the City Arms. Know it?'

'No.' She wondered why he was travelling by this route but she didn't ask.

'Of course you do. Everyone knows it. At the end of Southfield Road. Great pub. Plenty of students go there. Music, football, good food, you name it.'

'No. I can't remember ever noticing it. Don't know that part of Oxford very well.'

'Oh never mind. It's easy to find.'

'Is it?' Bev had no intention of going there. She wasn't a pub kind of person, nor was Rick.

'Course it is. Just ask anyone round there. Famous you see.'

'Right.' Where was all this talk going?

The blue eyes were closer now.

'I was wondering if you'd like to meet me there for a drink one night. Wednesday around seven?'

Bev's mouth fell open. She must be hearing things. Why would a younger man want to date a middle-aged woman? Even so, she felt as if she'd just been given a bouquet of red roses. She wanted to hear him say it again. Music.

'That's very kind but I'm married,' she lied. 'With a daughter.' She looked at her wedding ring as if to make her point.

The words just fell out automatically. It was what she wanted to say. Or was it? She didn't know him. He didn't know her. She didn't even know his name but he seemed an honest guy. She hadn't wanted to hurt him.

'Fair enough,' he said, but he looked disappointed all the same. For a moment his body seemed to droop forward. After that he was silent and left at the next stop. It couldn't have been much more than five minutes that they had been talking.

Something unexpected had happened. One meeting on a short bus journey had lifted her spirits.

The blue and white blocks of the JR appeared, next stop was hers.

As Bev stepped onto the pavement, she thanked the driver for more than he would ever know, for her joyful journey. Someone wanted her. Someone wanted to be with her. Someone had chatted her up. Maybe she was still fanciable and not as past it as she had thought.

After all, the gardener-man had singled her out. Should she tell Amber and her friend that a man had tried to date her on the number 13 bus? She might. She might even tell Bert at the hospital. She often went next door for a cup of tea and he always liked to hear what she was up to. She knew he would tell her it was about time she met someone new.

'Your Rick's a fool leaving a lovely young wife and daughter.' Bert couldn't believe what he'd done. Kept on about it.

Maybe she would phone her parents and cheer them up. They were so concerned about her. She could just imagine her mum's face and that smile.

She could even check out the City Arms and who knows, meet up with gardener-man. Amber could come too and her friend, a girls' night out. Better still she could go on her own on Wednesday, about seven he said. She hadn't been out on her own at night since Rick left.

She slipped off her wedding ring and put it in her handbag. When she got home it could go in the box of memorabilia she kept in her wardrobe because that's what it was. In the past. It could join Amber's school reports, her first babygro, a small wedding photo album, her Gran's pearls, and stuff like that.

Rick wasn't coming back to her. Ever. They were divorced and he had a new family now. She had to get used to it and start living again. So many options were all crowding into her thoughts. She made her way to the hospital entrance and if anyone was watching her, they would have seen she was almost skipping along the road.

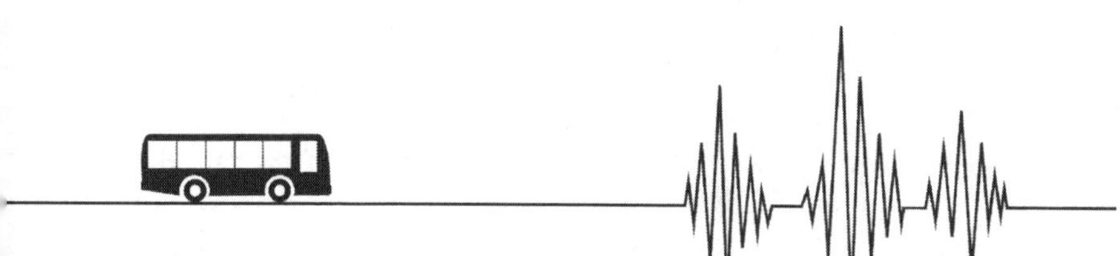

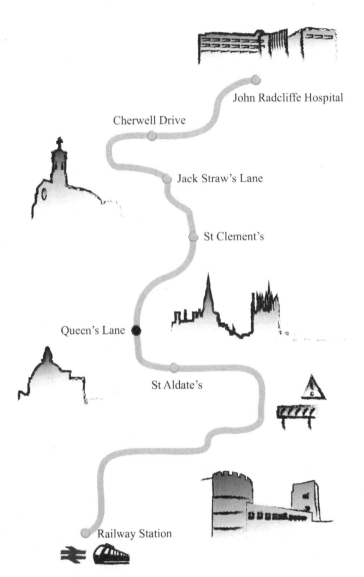

John Radcliffe Hospital

Cherwell Drive

Jack Straw's Lane

St Clement's

Queen's Lane

St Aldate's

Railway Station

Beyond her Grasp

HEATHER GELLES EBNER

Charlotte poured a strong cup of coffee, held the mug in her hands and inhaled. The heat and aroma were as much a part of her morning ritual as actually drinking it. She called to the children with an unmistakable, 'I mean now' intensity this time. Her husband, Tim, had already left for work and she would have to get them fed, dressed, and dropped off at school before catching her train to London for a full day of meetings.

'Coming Mum!' they both cried in unison, finally descending the stairs, having recognized the tone of the third call to breakfast. They plonked down at the table and reached for boxes of cereal. Charlotte ran through 'the list'.

'Make sure you have your tennis kit today,' she reminded her son. And turning to her daughter she added, 'Don't forget to hand in this permission slip, OK? It's for your school trip this Thursday.'

Two sets of semi-drowsy eyes and rumpled hair nodded agreement as they heaped spoonfuls of sugar into their bowls. Charlotte glanced at the time on the microwave, 7.15, and opened her tablet to check her email.

Her breath caught in her throat.

She re-read the message three times.

'Mum, you're not helping!' her son whined.

Charlotte's attention snapped back to the room, away from shock of the message. Her 7 year-old's wobbly grasp of a large container of juice was seconds away from spilling its contents all over the table and floor.

Charlotte swooped in to grab the carton in time but her hands were trembling. She barely managed to pour the juice into his glass herself.

'What's wrong with your hands Mum?' her daughter asked.

'Nothing sweetheart,' Charlotte reassured with practised effort, 'Everything's fine.'

But it wasn't fine.

Charlotte had learned to ignore these kinds of messages – messages from her mother, Rosalyn. Or to be more accurate, messages sent via whichever family member her mother had wrestled into service as an intermediary. Messages from Rosalyn were designed to capture attention; they were heavily embellished, laden with partial truths, exaggerations, and sometimes outright fabrications. As a result, it had become impossible for Charlotte to respond to them with the sort of compassion their content was designed to elicit.

Over the years, Charlotte and most of her mother's immediate family had become inured to the litany of ailments that 'suddenly' afflicted Rosalyn. Curiously, each ailment vanished just as suddenly as it arrived. Each medical drama seemed to occur rather too coincidentally with anyone else's good news. Charlotte could plot a timeline of her own important life events with the list of corresponding medical diagnoses which her mother had announced.

Her marriage to Tim – Lupus.

Her promotion at work – IBS and Chronic fatigue.

The purchase of their first home – Breast lump.

The birth of her son – Diabetes.

The arrival of her daughter – Glaucoma and Rheumatoid Arthritis.

Her recruitment and the move to Oxford – Adoption of a baby from China. (Admittedly, this one was a surprising turn. Nothing ever came of it. No-one had expected it to.)

There were almost-suicides and bouts of depression, along with various other minor illnesses too numerous to mention. When Rosalyn exhausted all the usefully vague medical possibilities, she would co-opt the illness of others. Charlotte remembered with a twinge of anger her mother's behaviour when her own brother had a very close brush with death. Charlotte's closest uncle was in a precarious state with his T-cell count plummeting to dangerous levels and Rosalyn had responded by taking a generous handful of tranquilisers, lying on the sofa and holding Charlotte hostage on the phone for over two hours. 'I just can't believe this is happening . . . to *me*,' she had cried. In Rosalyn's world, the crisis wasn't happening to her brother, it was happening to *her*. That explained everything you ever needed to know about Charlotte's mother.

And yet, this message seemed different.

Hi Charlotte,

I hope you had a good Easter. I know that lines of communication are strained so I just wanted to share some information with you, in case you didn't already know. Your step-dad, David, called Uncle Geoff this weekend (not sure why he didn't just call us directly). He said that your mother has been diagnosed with lung cancer – Stage IV. It has spread to her brain, spine and liver. I called the house and she was just back from hospital. David says that she is undergoing radiation for the brain tumour before chemotherapy for the rest. We thought you should know.
Love, Aunt Carol

This one was specific. Detailed. Not at all vague and woolly.

Was it true? Rosalyn had never smoked. But lung cancer had taken both Charlotte's maternal grandmother and grandfather.

The news felt heavy on her. Guilt, like a suit of lead, made Charlotte's every attempt to get on with the morning routine sluggish and clumsy. 'She'll want to see the children,' she thought. If Charlotte called, she would have their number. All the barriers would come down – just like Rosalyn wanted.

'I don't have time for this now,' Charlotte thought, determining to put it out of her mind for the moment. She packed the children's lunch bags and shuttled everyone out the door on time.

On the train to London, Charlotte considered how to respond to the message. Her insides churning with dread. She rang her husband Tim and, loathe as she was to have this kind of conversation within earshot of others, attempted to discuss the latest bombshell.

'Do you think it's legitimate?' Tim asked.

'I don't know.'

'You really don't know?'

'I . . . What if it isn't,' she began but stopped. 'She has done this before you know.'

'Well, who is the message from?'

'Aunt Carol'

'OK, she and Patrick have always been level-headed. You can trust them, can't you?'

'Can I? Just like I trusted my Dad when he insisted I visit her that weekend, just like I trusted my step-dad when he said she was bringing me home, just like I trusted her when I got into that car and ended up 2,000 miles from home. I don't trust anything when it comes to my mother. You know that.'

'I do. Well, what does your gut say?'

Charlotte thought about this.

'I don't know why, but I think it might be true this time.'

'That's very tough news if it is. How do you feel about that?' Tim asked.

'Not the way I'm supposed to feel.'

Her words were cold. She hated herself for saying them. Tim was the only person she could be honest with about it. And even then, she felt ashamed to admit this.

'Do you want to call her?' Tim continued.

'Well, what I *want* to do and what I *should* do are two different things. I don't want to pretend to express feelings that I don't actually feel.'

'You don't feel any sympathy for her Charlotte?' Tim asked.

Charlotte's voice rose slightly in defense, 'I'm not saying that. It's just that I don't *feel* anything. She obliterated what I used to feel. It's been years since we've spoken – you know that. And it has been peaceful without her in our lives – without the constant worry of what bomb she was going to drop next. I haven't missed her. I'm sorry it's like that but it's true. I haven't missed the drama and the problems. It isn't easy for me to re-kindle some kind of daughterly love. It just isn't,' she paused. 'Do you know what I mean?'

But feeling vulnerable, she didn't give Tim a millisecond to respond.

'Of course, *you don't* know what I mean. Because you have normal parents and a normal mother,' Charlotte sighed. 'I hate being put in this position. I sound heartless. This doesn't change what she did. You do know that, right?' Charlotte's voice was insistent.

'Sweetheart,' Tim said gently, 'I love you. Think about it a bit, then do whatever you think is best.'

'Ok, well, let's talk about it more tonight. Can you ask your colleagues at the JR for a clearer picture of what her outlook is – I mean, assuming this is real?'

'Absolutely, I'll talk with a few of the medics. Love you.' Tim hung up.

Charlotte wished she had bought a newspaper for the train journey. She was desperate for something, anything, to keep her mind distracted. It had been six years since Charlotte and her husband and two children had moved to Oxford. Before the move, calls from her mother were frequent, always bearing news of some personal crisis, real or imagined. It was a pattern which all of the family had come to recognize and with which everyone had found their own ways of dealing.

As the train rumbled along, the rain dripped down the windows. Charlotte recalled painfully a phone conversation with Rosalyn almost a decade ago before the move. So many of them rang along similar lines. Her mother had called at 8:30 in the morning – always a chaotic time back then as the children were just toddlers. Rosalyn was in the grips of another depressive episode evidenced by the gloomy voice.

'*Charlotte . . . you aren't busy are you?*'

'*Well actually . . .*'

'*I'm just having another one of those days,*' Rosalyn sighed. '*Everyone is so distant. Your Uncle won't call me back. He never picks up his phone and I know he's there. John's too busy at work and I just feel so down.*'

'*Mom, maybe you should go for a nice walk or something. Don't worry about Uncle Ray. He doesn't answer the phone when I call either, Mom. Just leave him a message, that's what I do. Uhm, but I kinda have to get ready for work now . . .*'

Charlotte tried to sound sympathetic but her responses had a hint of urgency – the cues that most interlocutors would understand as signaling the need to get off the phone and speak later either eluded Rosalyn or she chose to ignore them.

'*It's not just that, it's you Charlotte. Why don't you love me? What have I ever done to deserve all this?*'

Charlotte took a deep breath – it could be a long conversation if not handled carefully.

'*Mom, I do love you. I'm just a little busy this morning. I have a board meeting later and I've got to get the kids to nursery . . .*'

'*Too busy for your mother? Typical Charlotte. If you loved me you'd stay on and talk.*'

'*Mom, I just can't spare three hours on the phone all the time. I have to go to work and get the kids to nursery.*' Charlotte could feel her mother drain all the energy from her body – it took so much to stay positive in the face of her onslaught. Rosalyn's tone became more combative.

'*I don't ask for much Charlotte. Why are you so hurtful?! Why is everyone always hurting me? Are you trying to punish me? What did I ever do to you?*'

Rosalyn *had* done something. And she did know what it was. But she willfully chose to ignore it. Refused to admit she had done anything at all. As Charlotte tried to consider how best to side step this highly charged question, Rosalyn jumped in again, winding up for attack.

'*I never ask for anything! Never. All I want is to love you. That's the only thing I'm guilty of – I just love people too much.*'

'*Mom, why don't we talk about this some other time, OK?*'

'*You're avoiding me, aren't you?! Some days I just don't know if I can go on . . .*'

Charlotte could feel herself running out of patience. But she knew that the key to getting off the phone without further drama and headache was staying calm and being as non-confrontational as possible.

She answered quietly, '*I'm not avoiding you Mom. You were just here this weekend for dinner, right? I am in a rush because I have to get the children dressed and I have a presentation at work.*' As she said this, she thought to herself with some resentment that her mother had no idea what this was like. From the age of 3, Charlotte had grown up with her father; her mother had not gotten custody after the divorce, probably for very good reasons. Rosalyn never had to get a small child dressed for anything, she never cooked or cleaned her apartment, she rarely worked – and she had never been on time for a presentation or appointment or anything for that matter, ever.

In fact, even when collecting Charlotte for her weekend visits, Rosalyn could not manage to be on time. Charlotte doted on her mother back then. With a tiny posy of wild flowers and a crayon drawing of pink hearts for her Mom, Charlotte would wait and wait. Rosalyn would routinely show up *hours* late. Charlotte would sit with her elbows on the windowsill, face in her hands, staring out at each passing car light hoping it was her mother. The agony of all that waiting, the disappointment when Rosalyn sometimes failed to come at all – reminded Charlotte that the notion of needing to rush was simply beyond Rosalyn's comprehension.

'*Fine,*' Rosalyn snapped suggesting clearly that it was not fine.

Charlotte exhaled a long, deep breath, '*Listen, Mom. I won't be home until late tonight but come over this weekend and play with the kids. They'd love that.*'

'*Why don't you love me Charlotte, why? You never call . . .*' She trailed off crying and blowing her nose.

'*Mom, please, can we not do this?*'

'*I hope your kids don't treat you the way you treat me!*' Rosalyn said, her tears drying instantly with the heat of her rage.

'*I have a very different relationship with my children . . .*'

'*What the hell does that mean?!*'

Charlotte instantly regretted saying it – she should have known better. She was determined not to be sucked in but, as usual, her mother had pressed and pressed.

'*Don't be such a coward Charlotte. Say what you mean.*'

Charlotte looked at the clock, as the minutes had ticked by. At this rate, she would already be late to work. Any later and she was in danger of having to invent some outrageous explanation to excuse missing the first half of a board meeting. Whilst silently debating how to address the words that still hung in the air, Rosalyn jumped in again to fill the silence.

'*Well let me tell you something! You clearly have issues and you should see a therapist about that – because you clearly need to work on it!*'

Charlotte's reserve tank of patience was now on empty.

'*What?!*' Charlotte spluttered, '*I am the one who needs therapy?! That's interesting Mom – have you honestly forgotten the kidnapping?*'

And instantly, Rosalyn's voice shifted. It took on a syrupy, solicitous tone. Things were right where she wanted them now.

'*See, that's what I mean, Honey. It was a vacation. I don't know where you've gotten this idea about kidnapping in your head but you really should see a therapist about it.*'

Charlotte was fuming inside. She held the phone away from her and stared at the instrument of her torture. She resisted the urge to throw it in the bin and to give up all attempts to end the conversation in the normal fashion.

'*You still can't see it,*' Charlotte said with a tired voice. Holding the phone to her ear with her shoulder, she was trying to secure a shoe on her fidgety 2 year old. '*Your actions fundamentally changed our relationship. And you're still pretending that nothing happened. I can't help you with that.*'

'*But see, that's what I mean. You've just twisted events in your mind, Honey. You need to fix that so you can love me again,*' Rosalyn replied sweetly.

'*Mom, I'm perfectly content with our relationship the way it is. You're the one who can't accept it. Maybe you should see a therapist and work through your feelings.*'

'*Don't use that tone with me you snotty little bitch! You're my daughter, whether you like it or not!*' And Rosalyn slammed down the phone.

The truth was Charlotte's mother *was* ill.

Very ill.

And she had been so for most of her adult life.

But not with the litany of invented illnesses she convinced herself she suffered from. It was mental illness that plagued her.

Her mental health issues had been observed and diagnosed by dozens of psychiatrists and counselors. Each time one of them attempted to move beyond simple sympathetic listening and dared to encourage the hard work of self-examination, she would terminate the sessions and find a new counsellor. She refused to venture a single step along the path of self-recovery. 'I don't want to be challenged,' she had admitted to her brother in an unguarded moment, 'I know exactly what I need.' Rosalyn would occasionally take Prozac or Valium but the acceptance of any personal responsibility was absolutely out of the question. Everyone else needed to change, not her.

As a consequence, Rosalyn's siblings kept their distance. She had no lasting friendships – all of them eventually broke down, ending with Rosalyn utterly blameless and 'misunderstood'. Even her father found it difficult to engage with her though it pained him – 'she always seems to cause so much trouble.' How David had stayed with Rosalyn all these years, Charlotte never understood, although she was grateful. Without her step-father, more of the burden of care might well have fallen on her as the only child. Charlotte found the best thing for the sake of normalcy was to maintain a clinical detachment – shutting Rosalyn out completely only made her more desperate and rash – Charlotte simply kept her mother emotionally at arm's length.

The final straw, however, had come a year after their move to Oxford. It must have been one those desperate crises for Rosalyn. She had decided she *had* to speak with Charlotte but her timing was unfortunate. It was a week before Christmas and Charlotte and Tim had already packed up the kids and were on their way to Florida to see Tim's family.

Rosalyn really lost it.

She had phoned Charlotte's work, her house in Oxford, and then every relative she could think of, trying to 'find' her. Rosalyn had eventually rung her ex-husband, Charlotte's father. He explained that the family was in Florida for Christmas and then, rather reluctantly, provided the in-laws' number.

By the time she phoned Tim's parents' house, Rosalyn had worked herself into an emotional frenzy. She had shot straight through sadness and tears, on to outrage and threats before she had spoken to a soul. While Charlotte and Tim were out shopping with his parents, Rosalyn had left this voice message:

'Hello?! Well, fine. Pretend you're not there. This is Rosalyn. I'm sorry to do this Mrs Schafer, but since I can't seem to reach Charlotte directly, my attorney will be serving her with papers. I will not be kept away from my grandchildren! I have rights and I'm taking them. I suggest you have Charlotte call me immediately.'

It was horrible.

Gut wrenching.

Embarrassing.

And, especially for Charlotte . . . absolutely terrifying.

What she heard in Rosalyn's bellicose, slightly unhinged voice on the answer machine was: *'I'm going to take them, just like I took you.'*

She had seen her mother go off the deep end before.

Been on the receiving end of it.

Knew the warning signs.

Tim had replayed the unbelievable voice message again, whilst his parents looked on with awkward shock, Charlotte had stood frozen, a cold bath of fear washing over her. She was transported through time and space. She was 14 again; Rosalyn was screaming at her, yanking phone cords from every room so she could not call her father, she was hitting, clawing, raging at Charlotte and, then lying sweetly the next day, pretending to drive Charlotte back home as she locked the car doors. A 45-minute journey stretched into hours and then days as Rosalyn sped past one state border after another. It had been the most harrowing ten days of her life. Charlotte's ears were ringing and hot as she stood in her in-laws kitchen. All she could hear was the sound of her mother's cold voice 20 years earlier, *'If you don't calm down and stop that crying, I'll give you a tranquilizer.'*

Charlotte knew exactly what Rosalyn was capable of.

The flashback flooded through, chilled her to the core. And that voice, that message, froze any remnant of love that had remained into an icy stone.

When they returned to Oxford, Charlotte changed their phone

numbers, bought a new cell phone, instructed the children's school (embarrassing as it was) that if some woman claiming to be their grandmother showed up she was not permitted to take them from school under any circumstances.

They even moved house. Within a few months, Rosalyn no longer possessed any valid contact details for her daughter, Charlotte or her grandchildren. If she had thought that bullying threats would prevent Charlotte from depriving her of access to the grandchildren, she had made a misjudgement. It had, in fact, secured that very outcome.

Though Rosalyn persisted in her attempts to reach them, her efforts gradually lost intensity. A year later, the only contact that remained consisted of occasional email messages from family members bringing news of Rosalyn's 'illnesses' – mostly imagined. From time to time, Rosalyn would become irate with her messengers for refusing to give over Charlotte's contact details. Insisting she needed to speak to Charlotte directly. Why was everyone treating her this way? She railed. What had she ever done to deserve this?

When guilt failed to persuade, she reverted to threats – but still she was firmly rebuffed. The entire family honoured Charlotte and Tim's decision to keep Rosalyn at arm's length. Until the children were grown. Charlotte's aunts, uncles, and even her grandfather, remembered Rosalyn's off-the-rails kidnapping and felt uneasy; unable to completely rule out some future attempt at an encore. Under strict orders not to divulge any details with Rosalyn, the family kept their word.

Charlotte was beyond her grasp.

The train had emptied while Charlotte was still lost in her thoughts. A chap from First Great Western was making his final sweep through the carriages and briskly shooed her out. Apparently she was the last passenger off the train; if Oxford hadn't been the final stop, she would have missed it completely. She barely remembered any of her meetings in the City. All she had thought of all day was the email message from her aunt. She stepped onto the platform, and hoped that Tim had cooked something for dinner though she suspected it was actually her turn.

Late in the evening, after several rounds of story-reading and tooth-brushing, followed by re-brushing *with* toothpaste, one more bedtime story, and a minor skirmish involving lights left on or off, the children were finally in bed. Charlotte and Tim resumed their discussion. Though she tried to think rationally about it, Charlotte was gripped by competing emotions. She did *not* want to contact her mother – it was a thing she was resisting not willfully but as if by some self-protective force field. And yet, she felt growing unease, an anxiousness, about her mother's supposed diagnosis.

Charlotte needed to know more. But she could not bring herself to call. She felt her defences weakening, but she knew that once she called Rosalyn, there would be no going back. She just wasn't ready to let her back in.

In the end, Tim sensibly suggested that they simply send some direct, medically relevant questions that would flush out the truth and, if truth it was, flush out the severity. Her aunt had passed them on (without attribution) and agreed to report back with news. The week rolled by in a blur. Children still had homework, laundry still needed washing, and work in the College still demanded Charlotte's full attention. The veneer of normality was maintained. But Charlotte's worry was deepening. With each passing day, the ice was beginning to melt.

By the weekend, she decided to phone her uncle. He had always understood and shared Charlotte's frustrations with his sister and had therefore always served as a good barometer of these situations. He had just been to the house to see Rosalyn, he said.

It was real. Non-small cell. Aggressive. Undetected for months – silently hiding behind lifelong asthma and her burgeoning weight. Rosalyn was in good spirits, he said, in spite of the diagnosis; she seemed strangely happy. But, her uncle cautioned, the radiation treatment on Rosalyn's brain tumour was affecting her recall and it was difficult to talk to her sometimes.

'She won't bring up the past Charlotte, she's beyond that already or else she's not willing to risk arguments at this stage. She'll be glad you called if that's what you want to know. It will be OK.' Charlotte hadn't even had to ask him. He knew.

Two more days passed and finally, Charlotte collected herself mentally for the phone call she would make. David, her step-father, answered. It was a little awkward. She could hear his hesitation; they hadn't spoken in years. But behind the words spoken, she could sense the hurt, the worry, anger, and in some part, relief that she had called, all rolled together in his voice.

'I told her you would call. Did Aunt Carol tell you everything?'

'Yes,' Charlotte answered. 'She's been sending me updates by email. How much time is there?'

'I don't know – the doctors come in for five minutes and then they're gone all day. They aren't saying much. Could be two months, could be a year if the chemo goes well. But it's not curable.' The words were like lead. They dropped heavily to the floor and with them, his composure fell. David's voice was breaking up with emotion. Charlotte had never heard him like this before. She could barely understand him.

'Can I talk to her?' Charlotte asked, feeling she needed permission.

'Yes, but she's back in hospital now. Yesterday she lost vision in one eye – it might be the brain tumour, we don't know. She'll be really happy to hear from you but you better . . . prepare yourself,' he said.

'For what?' Charlotte felt a defensiveness rise in her throat.

'She's not herself Charlotte. She's, uh, having trouble remembering things. Just don't want you to be shocked.' He gave her the number for the hospital room and told her to call in an hour when Rosalyn would be eating. 'She'll be more alert,' he said.

It was 5 p.m. in Oxford when Charlotte phoned the hospital, lunchtime in New York. Her hand trembled and her dialling was clumsy, cumbersome. She could feel her heart pounding so hard it threatened to leave her ribcage, could hear it thundering away in her ears. She felt hot, felt the grip of panic squeezing. She held her breath as it rang. David answered and gave the phone to Rosalyn, saying 'It's Charlotte. I told you she'd call.'

'Well hello,' Rosalyn said in a sweet voice without a hint of anything beyond pleasant surprise. But the cadence of her voice sounded strange, not belonging to her at all – it was a voice that sounded entirely unfamiliar and Charlotte guessed that medication and various other interventions might be causing it.

'How are you Mom?'

'Well, no one can believe how fast this thing is moving,' she said referring to her own cancer matter-of-factly.

'I can't believe you've been secretly chain smoking Marlboros all these years?' Charlotte said making a joke, trying to lighten things for her and for her mother.

Rosalyn laughed. A deep belly laugh and Charlotte felt better.

They spoke for a short while but Rosalyn seemed to find each question more difficult to answer. She was coming in and out of lucidity; parts of their conversation making sense, other parts drifting off in strange tangents the way that dreams do. Rosalyn often lost her train of thought and sometimes latched onto the word for whatever was directly in front of her – unable to retrieve the word that she actually meant. In the midst of asking about what the grandchildren liked to read, Rosalyn replied, 'I remember you were a fast reader too. You always liked the, uhm, the uhm . . . chicken and coconut pie.' Her lunch tray had arrived. It was not a book title that Charlotte had ever read. After just 10 minutes of conversation, Rosalyn had cut it short. 'Well, I guess I better get going.'

She had *never* once ended a phone conversation in the entire time that Charlotte had known her. In fact, she had once carried on talking for so long in spite of continued yawns and pleadings of tiredness, that Charlotte had literally fallen asleep on the phone while Rosalyn lectured on. Now, suddenly, Charlotte felt bereft. Why did she want to go so quickly?

Their roles were reversed. Replying solicitously, Charlotte plied, 'OK Mom, but shall I call you again – tomorrow?'

'Sure. I guess so, if you want . . . huh? What did you say about the window? There's a dog in the window?'

David came back onto the phone.

'Charlotte, she's getting tired and I need her to eat something. I think all this medication is what's making her so out of it. Try calling tomorrow, she's more alert in the mornings.'

Charlotte put down the phone and felt a numb despair. *It's like she's already gone.*

Charlotte managed two or three more conversations with her mother over the next few days, each one as brief and as semi-lucid as the first. There were many more calls placed than conversations because Rosalyn was often sleeping or out of her room for tests. Sometimes, she was simply just too out of it to speak on the phone at all.

On Tuesday morning, with the children safely off to school, Charlotte made her way into work. It was both a blessing and a sad comment on the observational skills of her colleagues, that the only person who'd really noticed her strained smile the previous week was the Head Porter. Nothing escaped his attention but she declined his kind offer of a cuppa, 'Tomorrow . . .?' she offered a bit more cheerily, 'I'll bring cake . . .'

'Will you be baking that yourself then?' he asked with a grin, 'reckon I might be on a diet tomorrow.' Charlotte laughed. Bob wasn't fooling anyone; he hoovered up every crumb of the last banana cake she had brought to the lodge. He gave her a wink as she grabbed her mail from the pigeon hole before scurrying out again.

She stood outside the gates of The Queen's College waiting for the No 13 bus. Relieved that she had no London meetings this week, she could put in a relatively easy week at the college and she had time this morning to meet with one of the doctors at the JR. Her husband, as promised, had lined up a meeting for her with one of his medical research colleagues. The man Tim worked with not only researched new potential treatments, but was also a medic; he currently treated patients suffering from non-small cell lung cancer. Charlotte was desperate for more information, the kind her step-father didn't seem to have, nor be asking for.

As the bus approached the stop, Charlotte stepped forward in the queue. She had one foot on the bus and was about to board when her cell phone rang. Normally, she would let the call go to voicemail but under the circumstances she had to check. It could be Tim cancelling their meeting. It could be . . . something worse. The driver rolled his eyes and Charlotte let at least one passenger by whilst she tried to listen to the caller, not an easy task on the busy High Street in Oxford. She put a finger in the ear opposite the phone trying to block out the noise. It was her dad.

'Honey?'

'Dad? It's really early for you . . . What's the matter?'

'Have you booked your flight yet?'

'No'

'I think you should call David right away.'

'What? I don't understand why are *you* calling about it?'

'Well, David just called me; he didn't know how to reach you. He says they made a decision to bring her home from hospital yesterday. She's on oxygen now and he said the hospice is being contacted. He sounded . . . distraught.'

'Ok, I'll . . . I'll call him right now,' Charlotte said ending the call. She shouted, 'Do you mind?!' at the woman rudely pushing her forward while the people behind her tutted. Charlotte was still partially blocking the door to the bus.

'Are you getting on, luv?' the driver asked. Charlotte was staring at her phone searching for the number she desperately needed to ring. She looked up – slightly confused – as if too much input had been received. 'What? Oh, sorry,' she said.

Charlotte stepped off the bus and stood in the middle of the pavement, forcing people to manoeuver around her as she dialled David and her mother's home number. The phone rang once, twice, three times. It was torturous. Finally, her step-father answered.

'Hello,' he said quietly.

'David? It's Charlotte. My dad said you tried to reach me? What's happened? Can I talk to her?'

'Charlotte, listen, you're not going to be able to speak to your Mom,' he said slowly, pausing for air. The next sentence was so heavy that it seemed to take all of his strength just to push the words from his lips. 'Charlotte, you aren't going to be able to speak to her at all – she's gone.'

Charlotte heard these words and felt her world stop.

John Radcliffe Hospital

Cherwell Drive

Jack Straw's Lane

St Clement's

Queen's Lane

St Aldate's

Railway Station

Speedy Gonzales Tropical Storm

Janet Bolam

On a Thursday, Mrs Hemmingway gets on the number 13 on Cherwell Drive, regular as clockwork. I get on a couple of stops before and save her a seat.

'Afternoon, Mrs Riley,' she said as she parked herself next to me pulling her nylon bag onto her knee.

'Afternoon Mrs Hemmingway,' I replied.

'I've news,' she said in her blunt way. Well, she originally came from Dewsbury and they're all like that up there. We aren't that 'to the point' in Sheffield.

'What's happened now?' I asked. It was a week since we'd last had a natter.

'She's gone and done it this time.'

I took a pack of Murray Mints out of my bag and offered her one; I could tell this was going to be a two Murray Mints story.

'Well, you know I told you that Tosca and Iolanthe were due to be on heat at the same time? And Mr Turner had organized for that stud to come up from Essex?'

'Speedy Gonzales Tropical Storm?'

'That's him. Cost £1000 just to have him come and do what the Lord intended.'

'For that? I hope he did a good job.'

'Well both bitches are with pup, if that's what you mean. All we've had is puppy talk for weeks and weeks. Pure bred pups fetch over £500 each.'

I was astonished. 'I bet that buys a lot of Pedigree Chum.'

'In their heads they've spent the money three times over. Her Ladyship wants a jacuzzi and he wants a Land Rover so's it's easier to get the dogs to shows.'

Mrs Hemmingway cleans for Mrs Turner, or 'Her Ladyship' as she likes to call her and it's not all she calls her by a long chalk. Suffice it to say, the term 'mutton dressed as lamb' has been used on many an occasion. Mrs Hemmingway likes

Mr Turner well enough though, and it's really him who keeps the dogs. He has nine Kerry Blue Terriers that he keeps in kennels down their back garden. Mrs Hemmingway thinks it's cruel to keep them like that, but she's absolutely sure it's Her Ladyship's doing, not his. She's not a dog person. He's always off, up hill and down dale, taking his dogs to show and one of them, Troy Blue Mountain, came a close 3rd in his class at Crufts last March.

Mrs Hemmingway shifted in her seat and drew a Kleenex from her bag.

'Her Ladyship had another of her 'assignations' last night.' Well, we both knew what she meant by that.

'Mr Turner gone to a dog show, had he?'

'Went yesterday. An overnighter. Soon as he was out of the door, up turns Jarvis, bottle of summat bubbly in hand, slimy grin and dachshunds in tow. Right little yappy dogs they are; she won't have 'em in the house, so he lets 'em run riot up and down the garden causing havoc with the Kerries.'

'He's still on the scene then?'

'Has been since Easter. Anyway,' she continued, 'last night, all was revealed in more ways than one. As it happened, Troy was off colour, so Mr Turner decided not to show him after all, packs up his heckle and his peckle and comes back early.'

'Unexpected-like?'

'That's right, Mrs Riley. So Her Ladyship spins him some flannel to explain why Jarvis is slouched on the sofa smoking a cigar.'

'And did Mr Turner believe her?'

'He must of, because he invited him to stay to supper.'

'Awkward.'

'Well it doesn't end there . . .' Mrs Hemmingway stopped for a moment because a lad had got on the bus without enough money for the fare, but drama over, a woman with red hair got up and gave it to him.

'They've just finished their steak and chips when an unholy howl comes from the kennels. It turns out that Tosca has started to whelp. Well she wasn't due for another week, that's why they weren't ready. So it was all hands on deck, and then Iolanthe starts as well. So they drag out the whelping boxes and bring the dogs into the kitchen and carry on with their meal. These things can take time, you know.'

'You don't have to tell me! Our Carol took 12 hours and Dean took over a day.'

'But here's the thing, Iolanthes's first pup comes before they'd had their after-dinner mints. And it were a shock. They were expecting a pure bred Kerry Blue, but what they got was half ginger. And it were the same story with the other four; some had short legs, some had ears that were all wrong. And to make matters worse, Tosca's were the same. It were clear who was responsible for this little lot, and it weren't Speedy Gonzales Tropical Storm.'

I was puzzled. 'But aren't Kerries quite tall, like labradors?'

'Yes, and dachshunds have tummies that scrape the floor.'

'So how . . .?'

'That's hardly the point, is it Mrs Riley? Mr Turner didn't know where to put hisself he was so angry.'

'He'd put two and two together, I suppose.'

'And made five.'

'So did he take a swing at Jarvis?'

'You've been reading too much Mills and Boon, Mrs Riley. Jarvis slunk off and no more was said on the matter. No. Mr Turner was furious because Her Ladyship let the dachshunds get to Iolanthe and Tosca in the first place. Lost him over £5000, plus the fees for Speedy Gonzales of course.'

'So not speedy enough.'

'Beaten to the post by Jarvis's yappy ginger dachshund. The pups are quite cute though. I think I'll ask Mr Hemmingway if we can have one.'

Mrs Hemmingway caught my eye and we got the giggles, laughed all the way to my stop.

'Well,' I said, wiping the tears away, 'see you next Tuesday.'

'Aye. See you then.'

John Radcliffe Hospital

Cherwell Drive

Jack Straw's Lane

St Clement's

Queen's Lane

St Aldate's

Railway Station

No Better Friend

ANNIE WINNER

They sat on the bus in a tense silence as it slid away from the station stop, bumping over the humps in the forecourt. June's hair, freshly dyed a red almost as unreal as the colour of a highlighter pen, flopped around her face as she settled herself into the seat. Barbara's hair was stony white and at first glance they looked like mother and daughter, but undistracted by the straight lanky red locks, you could see they were sisters, sharing the same straight nose and, now sagging, face shape.

Barbara's head was buzzing with the news of what she labelled June's latest escapade, although strictly speaking, it wasn't even hers, but her feckless, irresponsible daughter's. What June had just told her, as the train drew into Oxford station, felt like history repeating itself. Again. Then, the second hand grenade, lobbed as they had been standing outside the station waiting for the bus, had precipitated Barbara into exclaiming: 'You, you've been nothing but trouble since the day you were born. You're a complete waste of space, and so is that daughter of yours!'

The other people in the bus queue had stirred expectantly. Barbara realised that now was not the time to embark on the tirade that was bursting to be launched, hence the stand-off as they sat in the front double seat.

June sat with tears in her eyes, her throat constricted with misery and guilt. She pulled out a tissue and sniffed loudly. Barbara shrugged and stared doggedly out of the window. The bus trundled on and, unable to tolerate the stand off, June took out her phone and started texting.

'Put that bloody thing away!' hissed Barbara.

'Don't treat me like a ten year old,' retorted June.

'Well, you're behaving like one.'

June saw that one coming. She'd heard it before. A million times. The bus jolted to a stop in Speedwell Street; the driver

61

lowered the step and a young woman pushing a buggy manoeuvred it into the space in front of the sisters. June looked at the baby in it wistfully and said: 'Well, what am I supposed to do? Never speak to her again? She's my daughter for god's sake. She can barely cope with little Jaydon, let alone with a baby as well. When I had her, none of you lifted a finger to help me, and I'm not going to let her go through what I went through.'

'Well, you'd made your bed.' Barbara was beginning to calm down now. She smoothed her black coat over her knees and reached into her bag, retrieving a packet of Refreshers. She offered a conciliatory sucker to her sister.

'God, haven't seen one of these for years. He,' June paused, 'old shit-face, used to buy them for me.' Barbara stiffened again. The bus stopped in St Aldate's and several people got off, including the woman with the buggy.

'You've got no sticking power, June. Just because he's got a fancy woman is no reason to chuck him out. Forgive and forget, that's what I say.'

June snorted.

'What the fuck do you know about it!'

She had raised her voice and the eavesdroppers on the bus looked studiously at the floor, straining to hear above the clatter and rattle of the bus bumping over all the pot-holes in the road. Barbara made a split second decision and hauled herself majestically to her feet.

'I'm not going to sit here and listen to your foul language.' She attempted to make a dignified transfer to the seat across the aisle but, as the bus suddenly lurched round yet another wobbling bicycle, she found herself hurled almost into the lap of a dapper little man sitting in the window-seat.

'So sorry,' she gasped.

'That's quite all right.' he said lifting his cap.

June stayed in her seat, tears rolling down cheeks tinted with black mascara. Her most faithful companion, her mobile phone, was in her hands again. At least playing Candy Crush distracted her from the anxiety, both about her daughter's and her sister's cold clinging to convention. She sniffed as snot joined her tears and fumbled in her bag for a tissue. When she'd agreed to Barbara's suggestion that they should visit their mother in the John Radcliffe Hospital, she'd known that would also give her the chance to visit her daughter who lived on the Northway Estate. And that would mean she could no longer put off telling Barbara what had happened.

By now they were trundling down the High Street, one of the packs of buses that hunted the passengers waiting at the various stops. At the stop outside the Queen's College several more people got on, making the bus almost full. June glanced at them incuriously, too absorbed in her own misery to take much interest. After the bus crossed Magdalen Bridge and swayed round The Plain, the man Barbara was sitting next to indicated that he wanted to get off at the next stop. Barbara used this chance to climb down off her high horse and plumped herself back down beside June.

'So how are you going to manage?' she said. 'If Reg has moved in with his fancy woman he's not going to go on paying the mortgage is he?'

'You know quite well I've still got my job.' June was not going to let Barbara take the moral high ground again. 'And if you can't be helpful, just don't say anything.'

June felt stronger for trying to put a limit on what felt like a lifetime of Barbara's corrosive scorn. She could never live up to what Barbara described as "standards" so why try?

The bus stopped and started and people got on and got off, punctuating their jolting conversation. Barbara kept opening her mouth to say something, and then swallowed before it emerged. June would draw breath, ready to retort, only to find there was nothing to bat back. The other passengers who were close enough to hear above the inevitable racket were still straining their ears. One took off her hat so as to hear better; others examined their shoes, or stood up to re-button their coats.

Eventually Barbara took the plunge.

'Well what *are* you going to do? That job of yours won't even pay the mortgage and I don't suppose Reg will be too free with his wages.'

'I've been to the Advice Centre and they say we'll probably have to sell it, and split the proceeds.' She welled up again at the thought of losing her little house, but one good thing about the recent hike in Oxfordshire house prices was that they would make a good profit on the sale.

'But it won't be enough to buy even a flat, unless I can get a pay rise and a mortgage.'

Barbara was uncharacteristically silent. A horrifying thought started to creep into her consciousness.

'Are you sure you can't patch things up? It all seems so . . . so . . .' For once, she was lost for words. The more she tried to ignore what was more and more rapidly flooding into her mind, the more forcefully it had to be said.

'Well I hope you don't think you're going to move in with us. I've got more that enough on my plate what with Mum, and Tony working shifts and . . .'

June struggled to control the tears that were ever more urgently waiting to be shed. Mustering a brief salvo of sarcasm she said: 'Thanks very much for the offer but that would absolutely be my last resort. I'd rather be on the streets than putting up with your . . .' She couldn't think of the word, but the woman in the green dress sitting in front silently supplied it. 'Condescending patronage.'

Barbara felt both relieved and affronted. By now they had entered Marston Road where just after Edgeway Road a posse of Korean language students got on the bus, which was now full, and some of them were standing. At the next stop, one of them said:

'City Centre?' to the bus driver.

'No mate,' he replied.

'Where you go?'

'Hospital. Now move right down inside please.' The group started wittering and looked increasingly uncomfortable and confused.' Barbara couldn't resist coming to the rescue.

'You're going the wrong way,' she said. How many times had June heard that one? 'You want to get off at the next stop, cross the road and get the bus going back.' The spokesman looked bemused.

'Driver, stop and let these youngsters off!'

'They'll have to wait till the next stop.'

They duly did, and light dawned as Barbara got off the bus with them and pointed them to the stop on the other side of the road, just managing to hop back on, full of moral satisfaction at having done the right thing – again, thought June, who felt she never could. Barbara sat down next to June again.

'So what are you going to do? You'll have to rent somewhere.'

'Don't know whether I can afford it – rents in the city are so high now and further out, there's all the costs of travelling in to work. I was thinking . . .' she tailed off. She was half hoping that Sasha, her daughter, would suggest she moved in with her, but she hardly dared let that thought into her head. Besides, a two-bedroom council flat in Ploughman Tower on the Northway Estate with two small children did not fill her with enthusiasm.

'Well, what?' asked Barbara.

'Not sure yet.'

'What about trying somewhere you could share?'

June could hardly believe it. Barbara had actually made a positive suggestion instead of batting her down. She felt slightly disconcerted, she didn't know quite how to respond.

'Who with?'

By now, most of the passengers who had started the journey with them had got off, but the woman in the green dress in front of them was going to the hospital too, and she was enjoying the eavesdrop.

'Well I don't know,' said Barbara, 'but it must be nearly time for the students to be going off – you might be able to find a landlady, at least for a couple of months while you sort yourself out.'

'Well, it'll take that long to sell the house, at least, so not much point yet.'

'True.'

They fell into silence. June couldn't remember the last time they'd had even the shortest of exchanges talking as adults like this. Maybe it paid off to be a bit arsy with Barbara, like standing up to bullies.

By now they were through the residential area off the Marston Road and crossing into the Northway Estate – more neat rows of semis that June knew she would never be able to afford. A scruffy looking young man got on the bus. His gaunt face with 3 days stubble looked out from inside his hoodie. He searched clumsily through his threadbare rucksack and came up with a 50p piece.

'I need to get to the JR,' he said.

'Sorry mate, but it's £1.50.'

'But that's all I've got.'

'Well you'll have to walk.'

He looked so crestfallen and so desperate that before she could think June jumped up and laid the one pound coin she kept in her pocket on to the driver's counter. She knew what it felt like to be down to your last 50p'

'There' she said. 'That'll get you there.'

The young man looked at her with an expresssion of hostility mixed with incredulity. He opened his mouth, mumbled his thanks and shuffled his way to the back of the bus, trying to make himself invisible on the back seat, next to a tearful looking woman who was dabbing her face with a tissue.

'Well, I don't know why you did that,' said Barbara. 'He's got no business getting on a bus without the proper money. And did you get the smell as he passed by? I've no time for these wasters – he's probably on the dole too.'

June sighed. But she felt good about helping the man and she wasn't going to invite yet more stick from Barbara by getting into another argument. They both gazed out of the window at the neat semis on the Northway Estate. Barbara suddenly said: 'Well what about that shameless daughter of yours? You said you were going to stand by her, why not really help her out and move in with her?'

June was immediately thrown back into her usual role. But this time she wasn't going to have it. Instead of bursting into tears or shouting back, she said coldly: 'That's the last time you *ever* talk to me like that, Barbara Evans. I'm getting off here and I'm going straight to Sasha's. You can go and see Mum on your own. And you can ring me when you've learned how to speak to me with a civil tongue in your head.'

As the bus pulled up at the next stop she got up, stepped down from the bus and started walking – striding – purposefully along the pavement. As the bus passed her she caught a glimpse of Barbara's profile, staring fixedly ahead. June glimpsed a large tear rolling down her left cheek and realised that she had never seen her sister cry in all her forty years. Perhaps things had shifted.

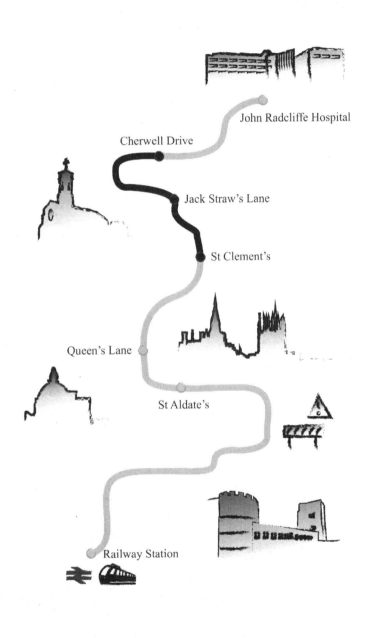

John Radcliffe Hospital

Cherwell Drive

Jack Straw's Lane

St Clement's

Queen's Lane

St Aldate's

Railway Station

The Gardener

NEIL HANCOX

S am and his tankard of ale were trapped between a woman
in her mid twenties, with an angular nose, and the bar. She
clutched a glass of vodka in her right hand. Her hair hadn't
seen a comb recently and darting bloodshot eyes were trying to
hide behind thin lenses in thick black frames, as though they
were ashamed of their owner.

'What have you done with your life?' she said in a slurred
voice. Another gulp of her drink and she answered for him,
'Not much.'

The beer was just the right temperature and he had been
enjoying a solitary drink before she had buttonholed him. He
was like his mother he supposed – people would suddenly start
conversations and tell him about their lives or, in this case, his.
His present life he enjoyed and he didn't wish to be reminded
about some of his earlier times. This woman was starting to
make him uneasy.

His attention drifted to a puddle of beer spilt on the
counter. A marauding fly had just landed and was having
difficulty freeing itself. Normally Sam had little sympathy with
insect life; they attacked his plants but in this case he would
make an exception. At least if the fly died it would be with a
smile on its face.

'Well?' the woman demanded thrusting her glass towards
him, annoyed at being ignored.

A companion intervened. 'Come on Amanda', a male voice
commanded.

She glared at Sam as she was steered away by a firm hand on
her elbow; probably looking for another victim Sam thought.
The fly managed to escape, though its flight path was groggy.

Draining his glass, Sam decided that it was best to leave in
case Amanda returned; time to navigate the fine web of small
streets on the Iffley side of the Cowley Road. In No.19,
Bronson would be waiting to welcome his master. The old

hound would bark once, wag his tail and amble up to Sam, hoping for a treat. The vet had recommended a scratch on the head instead but Sam was soft-hearted. Man and dog had been mates for eleven years so it was a toss up between longevity and pleasure.

Bronson did as predicted. Sam let him out into the back yard and settled down with a mug of coffee and the crossword before bed. There were problems tomorrow; not bugs and slugs with a liking for green shoots, and not the client. It was mechanical, his van was beset with rust and needed extensive welding before it was granted an MoT certificate. Public transport was not the place for paving slabs, spades and bags of compost. He would have to concentrate on planning and estimates.

Three across, seven letters, 'Away with you, I say indefinite article.' Begonia. He yawned, made sure Bronson was back in his basket and went to bed.

The first visits would be towards Marston and the John Radcliffe. Reasonable respectability was required on these occasions; clients liked to see smartish dress, strong working hands and a hint of dirt under the nails. He could oblige on all counts. As a concession to modernity he had a new shoulder bag containing his iPad and a laser measure. 'With these, Bronson, I can draw up a plan and superimpose images of any flower combination while you wait.' Bronson tried to wag his tail. Sam wondered if he needed an MoT, only the verdict might be . . . He shuddered and patted the dog's head.

Sam didn't feel in the mood for cycling. He walked across from the Cowley Road to St Clement's, to the bus stop by the Thai restaurant he sometimes visited; let the professionals take the strain of negotiating Oxford's traffic.

As Sam waited for the bus he went through his mental check-list. Men liked deference; if they maintained it was a lupin and in reality it was larkspur you needed to let them down gently; older women should be complimented and allowed to mother him slightly, younger ones, if the partner was absent, might like a mild flirtation. 'These were not skills taught in horticultural college or university.' Several people looked at him and Sam realised his thoughts had escaped into words.

He purchased a single bus ticket – no knowing what the day could bring. There were plenty of seats but he was in a sociable mood and chose to sit next to a middle-aged woman with nice hair and unpainted toe nails poking out from her sandals.

'Mind if I open a window?' he asked.

'No, please do.' It was probably those naked toe nails making him think she was warmer than she felt.

'Going to the JR?'

She nodded.

'You're not ill I hope?'

He was a stranger and this was approaching the personal though not offensive. He tried to sound concerned.

'Just visiting.'

Soon they were talking about trees. 'I'm a gardener and garden designer,' he offered by way of explanation, 'and I might be doing some work up at the hospital, greenery helps the healing process, you know.'

A stop or so passed and their conversation died away.

'Do you know the City Arms, in Cowley?' he suddenly asked her.

'No.'

'You ought to try it, lots of music, good food and lively students.'

'I often go along on a Wednesday, sevenish. How about meeting me for a drink there one evening?'

She shifted in her seat, trying to make a small gap between them.

The bus stopped and a noisy crowd of language students invaded.

'That's most flattering,' she said, adding, 'I'm a married woman with a daughter.' She proffered her wedding ring to reinforce her words. 'So I don't think so.'

He seemed slightly deflated for a moment; then sighed and smiled.

They were approaching Marston. 'My stop,' he said. 'Think it over, bye.'

As Sam thanked the driver he wondered what had possessed him. His fellow passenger was a pleasant soul; he could have sat anywhere; perhaps it was her distinctive floral top that decided the matter. Was it kismet, karma, fate? He wasn't too sure of the difference. It was done now; think gravel, shrubs, perennials that thrived on a lack of attention and a dearth of rain in the summer.

The first address was a 1930s semi with a surprisingly large front lawn that had yet to be converted to hard standing. The owner was another middle-aged, plump woman, wearing a distinctive floral top. Synchronicity? Sam was not a fashion expert; maybe floral was the in thing at M&S.

The woman asked him into the lounge and offered him coffee. While he was waiting he saw the graduation photo; the girl was in a gown and *sans* glasses, but there was no mistaking the angular nose – Amanda. There was another photo of an Amanda in mufti holding hands with the man from the pub. This was getting spooky.

He accepted the mug of coffee, assured the lady of the house that he did not want sugar, accepted a chocolate biscuit in lieu and steered the conversation round to the pictures.

'My daughter Amanda,' the woman said proudly.

'And her husband?' he asked artlessly.

The face became disapproving. 'No. He's Mr Indecisive, one of nature's lesser creations. When I think of all the things I've done for that girl, it was a struggle at first, she was three and a half when we adopted her. I'm sorry,' she said. 'It gets to me at times, especially since my husband went.'

Sam wondered why she had been deprived of her husband. Was it the Grim Reaper, grim daughter or even grim wife?

'Now about re-modelling my garden.' The words brought him back to the present.

He measured, sketched, superimposed pictures of flowers and omitted to say that they rarely looked so good in practice. She was convinced that he could make a difference and he agreed to start work in a few weeks.

The rest of the day was boring, completed while he was on automatic pilot – too many coincidences, too many confidences. Perhaps I should try a new career, he thought; Agony Uncle. Bring your problems to Uncle Sam; no that wouldn't do, he would need a new name, Adam sounded good. And he could include gardening advice. Dear Uncle Adam, My daughter is dating a most unsuitable older man and my garden is plagued with ground elder. What should I do? Answer; a good systemic weed killer will remove both.

The car blasted its horn. 'You silly sod, choose someone else's car if you want to commit suicide, I don't want my bodywork dented.'

Time to seek the safety of the pavement along Old Marston road and take a bus home.

It was Wednesday. He was tired and would like an evening at home but he had suggested a meeting with the woman on the bus last week, so he had better go to the pub. 'You can come along this time Bronson; see if you approve.' The dog looked at Sam's pocket. 'OK.' The treat disappeared in one gulp.

The City Arms was busy and he wondered if it was such a suitable meeting place. Too late; he ordered a pint of guest ale and a bag of ham and English mustard-flavoured crisps and managed to find a bench seat in the courtyard. He slipped Bronson's lead around a post and sat down to observe life and relax. Having observed and relaxed he pulled out his paper and tried the quick crossword. 'A flower, seven'. It wasn't aster or chrysanthemum. Sometimes these easy puzzles were harder than the cryptic variety.

'May I?'

He nodded without looking up and felt fingers take the crisp he was about to eat from his hand.

'Oh, hello.' It was the angry girl from the pub last week, the graduate from Marston. Now she appeared calmer; with steady eyes and well-groomed hair. He noticed that she didn't have a drink. 'Can I get you something?' he asked.

'No thanks, my fiancé is at the bar.' She hesitated. 'I recognise you from the pub last week; I'm sorry I was so rude. It was a very emotional time; I had only tracked my birth mother down a few months ago, and ten days ago she suddenly collapsed and died.'

'I am so sorry to hear that,' he replied. 'Please forget all about last time.'

The woman pulled a photo from her bag. 'That's her,' she said thrusting the picture at Sam.

It was a creased image of a girl in her late teens. Something deep in Sam's memory began to move. Now he was a member of the bourgeoisie, a pillar of contemporary society – he read a broadsheet, seldom exceeded the speed limit in his van and had voted for the Green candidate at the last local election. In his teens, however, that disturbed period twenty odd years ago, he had been on the outermost fringes of youth culture.

The fiancé arrived. Sam excused himself and Bronson wondered if he would be offered the remainder of the crisps.

Tomorrow was a busy day. Time for a mug of coffee and a relaxing clue or two.

First, though, he must unearth the canvas bag of family photos. There it was a small, faded, snapshot of a thin teenager, face framed with long dark hair, with his arm around the shoulders of an equally skinny girl. The angular nose had not been her best feature but he loved it at the time. His hair had gone but he had just seen a face that was similar; what might have been . . .

'Bed time Bronson.'

The dog growled.

'OK one last clue then. 'Mother's fateful transport.'

'What do you reckon, Bronson, Karma?'

But the dog was asleep, head resting on two outstretched front paws.

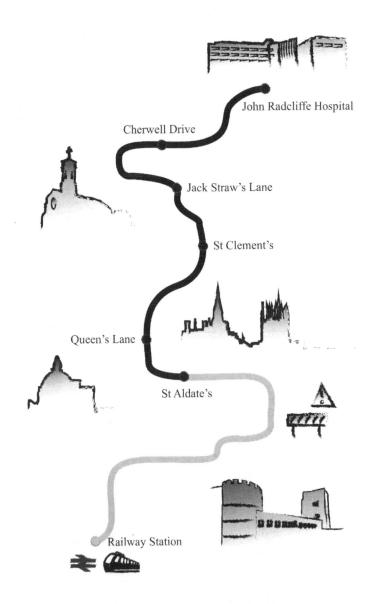

John Radcliffe Hospital

Cherwell Drive

Jack Straw's Lane

St Clement's

Queen's Lane

St Aldate's

Railway Station

A Comely Wench

ANDREW BAX

Penny was woken at 6.30 a.m. by a reedy, warbling noise that seemed to be coming from the road outside. At first she thought she was dreaming but as consciousness asserted itself she recognised something familiar about the sound. Fully awake now and with sudden anger she threw off the duvet and made for the window. Yanking open the creaky old sash she leant out and shouted:

'Oliver Prentice! Stop making that infernal racket. NOW!'

But Oliver did not stop. In fact he was struggling to reach a high C in a series of 'Fa la las' that are a common feature in many English madrigals. He was something of an expert in them.

He paused long enough to call: 'Happy birthday, my love.'

'I am NOT your love. You just want me to wash your smelly old socks.' But only the neighbours, roused by this early morning commotion, heard her because Oliver was into a new verse:

> Come away, sweet love, and play thee
> Lest grief and care betray thee

'Have you any idea how ridiculous you look?' It was true. Oliver did look ridiculous in purple doublet, hose and a floppy hat, strumming discordantly on a lute.

> Fa la-la-la la la

'You look absolutely ravishing, my dear.' Penny Archer glanced down and realised with horror that she was wearing her skimpiest nightdress and her hair, normally so immaculate, was hanging in tousled strands. She slammed the sash shut.

> Leave off this sad lamenting
> and take thy heart's contenting

77

She sat on the edge of her bed, seething. It had been like this for six months now. Oliver Prentice, recently abandoned by his wife and coasting towards retirement, had taken it into his head to embark on some kind of medieval courtship. He had even written to Penny's elderly parents, formally requesting their permission to woo her. The letter was written as a scroll on parchment, and they had to pay a surcharge on the postage.

Fa la la la-la la-la la la

Penny, herself, had a bitter experience of marriage and had resolved to have nothing more to do with men. There had been moments, of course, when her life, her bed and her little house in Grandpont seemed empty. There had been times when a sign from her could have brought men to refill the space but, resolutely, she spurned all overtures. There were also times when she rather wished she didn't. But the thought of offering any encouragement to Oliver Prentice only filled her with horror.

The nymphs to sport invite thee
and running in and out delight thee

She could just see him between the wall and the curtain's edge. He was standing in the middle of the road, making exaggerated gestures and singing in his high tenor towards her bedroom window. This would keep the gossips going for weeks. A car was approaching and Oliver stepped aside with a sweeping bow to let it pass.

Fa la-la, fa la-la, la la, fa la la

At last the performance came to an end. Oliver, silent now, was still standing in the road, looking expectantly up at her bedroom. In the good old days, she giggled to herself, she would have thrown the contents of a chamber pot at him.

Finally, despairing of a response, he called, 'Farewell, Penny, my love, till we meet again, adieu' and with that, he mounted his bicycle and rode off, oblivious to the spectacle of his preposterous outfit. Almost anywhere, apart from Oxford, she sighed, such eccentricity would attract attention but here, no-one seemed surprised. She almost felt sorry for him.

'Till we meet again.' Those words angered Penny almost as much as the madrigal episode, because they *would* meet again – in a couple of hours. They worked in adjacent offices in the Department of Cultural Anthropology. She was tempted to take the day off but her colleagues would be disappointed because they knew it was her birthday, and she had to deal with some late applications for a local seminar on *Celtic Influences on the English Canticle*, which the Department was hosting the following week. In any case, she had already arranged for an extended lunch break so that she could go to the John Radcliffe. She often went there to participate in a clinical trial but this time, although no-one else knew it, it was for a job interview. It was for quite a senior position with good prospects for advancement. It would mean a considerable increase in salary and she could get there easily by bus. Above all, however, it would mean she could get away from the odious Oliver Prentice.

When, after 34 years of marriage, Oliver's wife walked out on him, he took little time in casting around for a replacement. Penny was an obvious choice, he decided. Her rise from secretary to administrator was recommendation in itself. She was capable and well-organised, qualities he lacked himself and, since her divorce, there wasn't a man in her life. He would be doing her a favour. Without waiting for her parents to reply to his scroll, the courtship began.

Penny was appalled. She found nothing attractive in his fleshy lips and piggy eyes – or his sheer arrogance in assuming she was his for the asking. But, at the Department's Christmas party he managed to corner her in a clammy embrace. If only she had kept clear of the cocktails, she had told herself many times since, she would have fought back harder.

For Oliver the incident only encouraged him to believe that perseverance would pay off. The thought that Penny might not actually want him had not occurred to him. In any case, in true medieval fashion, he considered her thoughts on the matter to be a mere refinement. He did worry, though, that he had not had a reply to his scroll and, as he cycled home, he considered how the matter would have been addressed in the Age of Chivalry. Probably with a herd of swine, he thought, but that could be misconstrued. Perhaps oxen? Then he remembered that Penny's parents had limited grazing space. If animals were the answer, he decided, it should be a goat.

Penny took more time than usual in getting ready. She was careful with her appearance and much of her discretionary income was spent on clothes, shoes and handbags, and today she was determined to look her best for the interview. After coffee and muesli, she was ready for the short walk across Folly Bridge and into St Aldate's.

Opening her front door she discovered that Oliver's humiliation of her had not ended with the madrigal. Propped up on the doorstep was a huge bunch of wilting red roses. Forty-three, she counted, one for each year. That ridiculous man had bought them the day before but didn't think to put them in water. Typical. She thrust them straight into the recycling bin and strode off to work.

To her great relief Oliver did not say anything when she arrived. She knew he was in his office because she could hear him humming. He hummed continually but only recently had Penny begun to notice it, and it got on her nerves. Imagine putting up with that all day! No wonder his poor wife left him. Today he added a few 'Fa la las', no doubt for her benefit.

Several people brought her birthday cards and the Head's wife presented her with a huge cake, which she had baked herself. They gathered round her desk for the ritual embarrassment of singing *'Happy Birthday to You'*. In the middle of it all Oliver emerged briefly from his office, raised a polystyrene cup of coffee and said 'prithee make merry' or some such medieval nonsense, but no-one took any notice.

People didn't take much notice of Oliver these days. He had been a member of the Department longer than anyone else and, though usually affable, he reacted with such fury when anyone asked what he was doing that they didn't any more. However, his activities, whatever they were, seemed not to be causing actual harm and in less than a year his retirement would deal with the problem without awkwardness. In fact, after much persuasion, he had agreed to lead a workshop in the *Celtic Influences* seminar.

But all this was typical of the fudge and compromise to

which the Department resorted when faced with the need to make decisions, and was one of the reasons why Penny had decided to look for another job.

Penny was a loyal, hard-working and highly-valued member of the staff and what she was now doing made her feel guilty. However, at 12.30 p.m. she got herself ready and walked the short distance to the bus stop further up St Aldate's, thinking about the interview ahead. It was, in fact, her third interview for the job and she had been led to believe that she had become the preferred candidate. The prospect of joining the ranks of NHS managers attracted her, even though they were usually blamed when anything went wrong. In the Department, people were mildly surprised when anything went right.

The bus wasn't long coming. Apart from a couple of women who were arguing noisily, the other passengers were the usual mixed bag. Most of them were absorbed in their smartphones and took little notice of their surroundings. Penny was just considering the curious fact that strangers wave to each other in boats but in buses they ignore each other, when a man got on and sat in the seat in front. He seemed a friendly sort and, unusually, struck up a conversation with his neighbour, a woman who was probably in her 50s but looked older. Penny couldn't help overhearing their conversation.

Casually he asked, 'Going to the JR?' followed anxiously by, 'Not ill, are you?' That was a bit direct, thought Penny, but the women seemed to take it all right. She was going to visit a patient. After a pause they began a conversation about trees and it turned out that he was a gardener. Another pause and he began talking about where he lived off Cowley Road, and a pub called the City Arms. Suddenly he said:

'I was wondering if you'd like to meet me there for a drink one night.'

Penny was stunned. He had only just met the woman. He didn't even know her name or anything about her – yet he had the gall to ask her out. She seemed old enough to be his mother and was probably happily married with six children. She certainly looked it. Penny would have hit him with something hard and sharp but the woman just stammered something about her daughter.

'Fair enough' he said, and got off at the next stop.

This was outrageous. Even her much-despised former husband, with all his multiple failings, even *he* showed a bit of decency and respect. What made matters worse was that the woman was not outraged herself. She just sat there, with a little smile on her face. Could this still be happening in 21st century Britain? The cause for equality was lost if there were still women who allowed themselves to be treated so casually.

Penny knew she was at her finest when riled. The condition sharpened her mind and enabled her to articulate her thoughts clearly and concisely. Exactly how to make the best impression at an interview. She was going to get that job and then she would put paid to Oliver Prentice, once and for all.

Meanwhile, in another part of Oxford, Oliver was cycling along a road of terraced Victorian houses, looking for number 39. There were times, increasingly rare these days, when reality forced him to take stock of his situation, and this was one of them. He realised he had overplayed his hand with the madrigal and that the goat idea, though amusing, would probably make matters worse. He had decided to visit Penny's parents in person.

It was Mrs Archer who came to the door. Her husband was watching cricket on television and gave their panting, perspiring visitor no more than a casual glance before turning the volume down, just a little. Oliver found he was having to compete for attention with Jonathan Agnew at Trent Bridge. Penny's mother on the other hand, was a nervous sort, and was anxious to know who he was and what he was doing there.

He was a senior member of the Department where Penny worked, he explained, at the forefront of study in social and cognitive organisation. He would be speaking on some important advances in next week's international conference on *Celtic Influences on the English Canticle*. He had admired Penny for many years and they had got to know each other intimately. 'One thing leads to another, you know how it is, Mrs Archer'. His situation had changed recently and he was now in a position to bring happiness and stability into her life. But they knew all about this, of course, from the scroll he had sent them.

Penny's parents looked at each other blankly. Scroll? What kind of scroll? Then her father remembered getting a cylindrical object in the post, for which he had to pay an excess charge. It seemed to be written in some foreign language and he was so annoyed by the excess charge that he threw it away. Oliver was mortified. Parchment was not easy to obtain these days. Attaching it to a wooden spindle proved to be surprisingly difficult and he had spent many, many hours in composing the text. True, writing it in medieval English was probably a mistake, but even so . . .

The wickets were falling like ninepins at Trent Bridge and as the last man came in to bat there were still 16 runs needed to avoid the follow-on. Aggers was in sombre mood and Mr Archer sat bolt upright on the edge of his seat, entirely focused on the television. The first ball was edged to leg for four. Twelve runs to go.

Concern for Penny's welfare had been a pre-occupation for Mrs Archer ever since the silly girl threw out that long-haired man from Blackwell's – she always had been so headstrong and now what was she doing? Living on her own with no-one to look after her, that's what. So although she didn't understand much of what Oliver was saying, he seemed to be offering Penny what she most needed – security. He pressed home his advantage with talk of his re-evaluation of primary sources. He also made casual reference to his 'modest legacy', neglecting to mention that it had long since been frittered away. She wondered if she should call him Professor.

But she still wasn't sure what to make of their overwhelming and over-talkative visitor. He didn't seem Penny's type at all. She was such a level-headed girl but he seemed off with the fairies, over the hill, too, and fat. Penny had never mentioned him although Oliver was now telling her about their 'close relationship'. She wondered if she could ask him his age, but it didn't seem polite.

'I was just telling your wife, Mr Archer, about the charming little celebration we had for Penny's birthday this morning.' Mr Archer, who had forgotten about his daughter's birthday, turned to him and blinked. 'She seemed delighted.' Two more singles in quick succession and then it was the end of the over. Ten runs to go.

'I surprised her with a little madrigal, you know'.

'A what?' asked Mrs Archer.

'Secular partsong of the Renaissance. It made her flush with such pleasure that I nearly fainted at her beauty. And, if I may say so,' Oliver was in for the kill now, 'I can see where that came from.' Now Mrs Archer flushed. 'Would you like to hear it?' Without waiting for her to reply he began:

> *Come away, sweet love, and play thee*
> *Lest grief and care betray thee*

On hearing this extraordinary noise Mr Archer turned to see Oliver struggling once again to reach a high C. He had seen some weird people in Oxford in his time, but he had never had them in his house before. He hoped he would be leaving soon.

> *Fa la-la-la la la*

The madrigal went on for rather a long time and seemed to be having a paralysing effect on the cricket. There were three no balls in the next two overs and the occasional single but the batsmen were still at the wicket. The tension had almost reduced Aggers to silence.

At last the warbling stopped and the cricket moved on. Oliver was now addressing Mrs Archer on the kind of life he and Penny would enjoy. He painted a picture of domestic bliss in which Penny furthered her career while he retired to his study. There was thinking to be done, theories to postulate. The world was waiting. At a loss on how to respond, Mrs Archer turned to her husband saying, 'That sounds, um, nice.'

Just then a sudden roar from the television, echoed across the country and by Mr Archer with an exultant 'Yes!' greeted a six into the grandstand. The follow-on was saved. Mistaking this reaction to events at Trent Bridge for affirmation that the Archers approved of his courtship, Oliver rose, shook each of his bemused hosts warmly by the hand and, with tears in his eyes, said, 'Till we meet again – adieu', and left.

Cycling back to the Department, he reflected with delight on the way things had turned out. He had always liked

Grandpont, situated as it was near the river and Christ Church Meadow, and Penny was an excellent cook.

The thought of food reminded Oliver that he had missed lunch so, having attended to that matter, the afternoon was well advanced by the time he got back to the Department. Penny was already there and, apparently, she had gone straight into the Head's office and closed the door. The speculation aroused by such a rare event was given added piquancy when Oliver was seen putting his ear to the key-hole. All he could hear was muffled voices but soon a scraping of chairs and approaching footsteps told him that the meeting was over.

The door opened to reveal Oliver kneeling with his arms outstretched and his eyes closed in rapturous entreaty. Opening them a little, he saw it was not Penny standing in front of him, but the Head, and he and the Head had history.

The Head considered Oliver to be an embarrassing liability and was exasperated by his unexplained absences; worse, when chance partnered them together in the inter-departmental bridge tournament they lost every rubber, entirely through Oliver's incompetence. Oliver considered the Head to be an impertinent upstart and resented his attempt to have him transferred to Archaeology; worse, when chance partnered them together in the inter-departmental bridge tournament they lost every rubber, entirely through the Head's incompetence.

Borrowing an expression which his daughter was fond of using, the Head bellowed, 'Dr Prentice, I've had it up to here with you. What in God's name are you now doing now?'

'I, er . . .' stammered Oliver, 'I was expecting to see Penny.'

'Penny? Penny, you say?' the Head often repeated himself when stressed, 'Penny is leaving us.'

Everyone within earshot looked at each other in alarm. Who would order cups for the coffee machine? Who would help with grant applications? Who would remember to water the plants? Oliver was so dismayed that his knees, already creaking painfully, gave way entirely and he collapsed in a heap. 'Penny? Penny leaving? She can't! When?'

He was answered by a shrill, determined voice, 'Now!' and Penny, her head held high and her shoulders back, stepped past the Head, over the sprawling Oliver, through the Department and out of his life.

From floor-level, Oliver gazed after her, open-mouthed as all his plans unravelled. He struggled to his feet with the help of the Head's new PA, dusted himself down and thanked his rescuer. He had seen her around, of course, but never quite so closely. As if for the first time he saw a smiling face and strong limbs.

In fact, she was quite a comely wench. Perhaps . . . maybe . . .

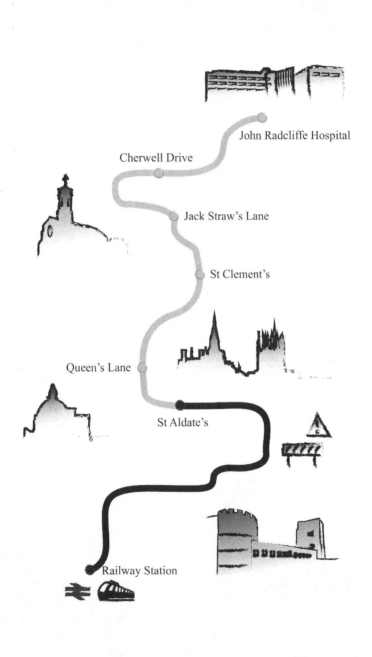

John Radcliffe Hospital

Cherwell Drive

Jack Straw's Lane

St Clement's

Queen's Lane

St Aldate's

Railway Station

The Gagliano

JACKIE VICKERS

Ana Hirsch, the violinist, has died unexpectedly in her sleep.

I had been her accompanist for the last twenty years and did not at first know how I should manage without her.

Some years ago, Sophie accused me of having an affair with Ana. I was deeply hurt. 'It is not that kind of relationship. What gives you that idea?' I said.

'There.' Sophie leaned over my shoulder and pointed to a photo in a music journal I was reading.

'That says it all,' and she stabbed a blood-red nail at the picture that accompanied a review of our most recent recital. I was sitting at the piano and Ana stood centre-stage in front of a rapturous audience.

'Look how she stands. Her public applauds, but she has turned to face you. And look at her smile. That smile is for you.'

'Of course Ana is smiling at me. That always happens. She is reminding the audience of her dependence on her accompanist. Without me she would be able to play only unaccompanied pieces, which would considerably restrict her repertoire.' I was being a little pompous, perhaps, but Sophie takes every opportunity to criticise.

She was no longer listening. 'When I see you together, I see that you have entered her mind, you know what she is thinking and what she is feeling. That is the kind of relationship you have, and it totally excludes me.'

Ana photographed well. She was small and slim with shoulder-length hair and big dark eyes. She looked much younger than her age, and I suspected that Sophie was annoyed by her look of eternal youth, rather than any emotional musical bond we had. From the beginning I had tried to explain how very difficult and time-consuming my work was, for Sophie had a very reductive view of musicians.

Musical ability, as she understood it, was merely a gift. She never recognised the necessity of so much practice.

'You play the same music every time,' she said, removing her glasses and giving me a long look.

'We have an extensive repertoire,' I protested. 'In any given season we play as many as forty different pieces.'

'I make forty different decisions every day,' Sophie snorted, putting her glasses back on to check the latest state of the Stock Exchange.

A few days later, Sophie had put her jacket on, arranged her scarf and hair to her satisfaction, grasped the handle of her suitcase and left. The wheels rumbled and her heels clicked down the tiled floor and out of the front door.

Ana had not seemed surprised when I told her. 'You should have married another musician,' she said.

Despite the large fees Ana commanded, she lived in rented accommodation in Headington, convenient for the bus to Heathrow.

'Owning property would give you security,' I suggested.

'My ability to perform is my only security. And if I lost that, my life would lose its purpose.'

'You would, at least, have a roof over your head.'

But for Ana, only music mattered. Once, when she failed to meet with our manager, I found her at home, still wearing her dressing gown, listening to old recordings by Isaac Stern and Ruggiero Ricci.

'These were the greats,' she said, wiping away her tears. 'Truly, Michael, I only fear one thing in this life and that is losing my hearing.' That she had lost her parents and her husband never troubled her.

'My mother and father lived long enough to see my success,' she shrugged, as though that was their sole aim in life. Perhaps it was.

But she spoke harshly of her husband. 'He had a limited emotional range. He smiled when I would have laughed. But worse, he found it unsettling when I cried over Oistrakh's recording of the Bach Chaconne.'

She gazed into the distance and I waited.

'So, I divorced him.'

'Over Bach?'

She smiled and took my hand. 'Listen, Michael, does music bring tears to your eyes?' And then I knew what Sophie's departure was about.

Ana owned a Gagliano, a nice Italian fiddle made by one of the better makers of the family – Niccolo. For recitals and concerts she had a Guanerius on loan from a rich and enthusiastic admirer. The Gagliano has a sweet tone but lacks the power of the Guanerius and is therefore better suited to chamber music and intimate venues.

'Did I tell you about my father's violin?' she asked every new acquaintance. 'My father had been a child prodigy,' she would explain in a husky voice, 'with quite a future before him. But he lived in a small village on the Polish border and when war broke out his parents urged him to flee. He was only twenty. The family was poor and had no transport so they strapped his violin to his back so that he was better able to run. It took him several days to reach the port and he had been badly injured in his left arm. Still, he made it onto the last boat to leave for England and safety. Many years later, when I began to show promise, he gave his violin to me.'

Her audience was inevitably moved to tears. But the whole story was a fairy tale. It had to be. Where would a poor family get a valuable violin from? Was it his teacher's opinion that his student was so talented and should be either given or loaned the violin? And if he was a prodigy, worthy of such an instrument, why had he not been sent years before to Warsaw, which has a fine conservatoire with scholarships for poor boys with talent. And on a practical level, how could he sit down on his journey with a violin strapped to his back? More important still, had the owner even agreed to his taking the violin away? In all other respects, she was a realist, she would always be cautious. If I were to suggest a small change to our programme, a more modern piece perhaps, to end on, Ana would always object.

'Tickets for our performances sell out in a few days, because we give our audience what they want to hear.'

'The public might like a change. I might like a change.'

'Now don't be temperamental, Michael,' she would laugh. 'That's my job.'

I found Ana's Gagliano story troubling. I wondered what an analyst would make of it. Did she have a deep-seated need to mythologize her family history? I never knew her parents, but I had often looked at the silver framed photo on her mantlepiece, which showed a pleasant-looking couple in their fifties standing side by side. Her mother wore black, her hair pulled back in a bun while her father seemed ill at ease in his suit, no doubt only worn for special occasions, as he was a watch repairer by trade. Neither smiled, though they looked kindly enough, if dull. It was difficult to imagine her father as a child prodigy or as a young man with an injured arm.

I asked her daughter Cecilia about the Gagliano one day. At that time I had been Ana's accompanist for some years and had already heard her story many times.

'My mother is a fantasist,' Cecilia replied, flicking her dark wavy hair back over her shoulder and giving me an inscrutable smile. 'That story is for the benefit of friends and fans, you know. She never mentions her Gagliano to me,' and Cecilia turned her attention back to her food.

Cecilia had studied music at the Guildhall School and had stayed on in London. I often thought it odd that Ana, who had many engagements in London, should live in Oxford, while her daughter, who could just as easily have built up her reputation as a teacher here, in Oxford, chose to live in the more expensive city. I put this to Cecilia, who laughed at me.

'But Michael, you live in Oxford!'

I had gone to London for the day and taken her out to lunch in a steak house; she had a robust appetite. Though now in her twenties, she retained a look of truculence, characteristic of her early teens. Her striking looks made heads turn wherever she went. I hoped the age difference was not too noticeable, for though I was too young to be her father, I might be thought rather too old to be dating her. And besides, I was then married.

Cecilia pushed her empty plate aside and to my surprise returned to her mother's story. 'I imagine you have noticed all the inconsistencies in that trek across war-torn Poland with a valuable violin. The wonder is that no one ever challenges her. Such is fame, it buys adulation, adoration and total devotion in your followers,' she said, raising an eyebrow. 'But, you see, I know the truth about this violin.'

'Truth?' I asked, refilling our glasses.

She sipped her wine, making me wait. 'My father had just left home. You know Ana divorced him?'

I nodded, 'because of Bach, she said'.

Cecilia rolled her eyes. 'As far as I understand there was no abuse, no adultery and no desertion, but my father was gone the day following that famous Bach episode, if indeed it ever happened. My nanny had taken my father's side, she said she didn't want to work for anyone so unpredictable and temperamental. My mother had not yet found a reliable replacement, so she had to take me everywhere with her, even concerts, rehearsals, shopping. I was only five and it was all such fun.'

'And was it fun?' I asked, amused at the idea of Ana, always so self-absorbed, having charge of a small child.

'Having my mother all to myself? I became the model child and, I have to say, she became for those few weeks a model mother. I remember little about my father or my nanny leaving, or my first months at school, but I do remember everything else about that Easter, the warmth of the sun, new sandals, the smell of lilac.' She laughed, 'well, maybe not the smell of lilac.'

Cecilia, animated, presented a delightful picture. The wine had brought a blush to her cheeks and a sparkle to her eyes. She wore a low-cut semi-transparent blouse, which gaped as she moved. As Sophie usually wore city clothes on the rare occasions we met for lunch, I enjoyed the contrast.

'It was the first time I had been on a train,' and Cecilia flicked her hair back again. 'I remember walking up a hill through woods. There was a village green with ducks and we went to the shop for bread to feed them. Then we went to a large old house hidden by fir trees.' Cecilia gazed into her glass, twirling the stem. 'I had to sit very still while my mother played different violins. I don't recall how long we stayed, but in the end she bought one and took it home.'

'But what makes you think it was the Gagliano?'

She looked up at me. 'Same case. And one day, a few years later, I squinted into the sound-hole and read the label. "Niccolaii Gagliano fecit in Napoli 1760". She had just put the violin in its case but left the lid up and went to answer the phone. That was very unusual, she kept an eye on it all the time.'

'I wonder how she could have afforded it so early in her career.'

Cecilia shrugged. 'Inheritance? Grandparents had died the year before.'

'Did you never envy Ana having such a violin, when she also had another for concerts? After all, you too play the violin.'

'But I'll never be a soloist, like her. The instrument I have is good enough for teaching. My mother has surely mentioned that I now have quite a number of promising students.' She leant back in her chair and, looking as she must have done aged five on that spring day, she raised her eyebrows.

'Are we having any pudding?'

I found Cecilia's story extraordinary, though I wasn't sure it was any more likely than Ana's. Ana always suggested her parents had lived modestly, it wasn't likely she would inherit such a sum. Then I wondered if her husband had paid her off in some way. Did he want out of the marriage, rather than the other way round, and was the Gagliano his price for her agreement? Then again, she may have taken out a massive bank-loan to pay for the violin, which would explain her reluctance to take out a mortgage. I never spoke to anyone about my theories, not even Sophie. I did not wish to give the impression that I was obsessed by this apparent puzzle in Ana's life.

And there it should have remained, as a puzzle for a rainy day. But then Ana asked a favour of me.

'Michael, dear. Would you take my violin next week? Cecilia usually does, but she is going away.'

'But Ana, I can't guarantee its safety,' I protested.

She was going into The Manor Hospital for one of her endless investigations. Perhaps it was a way of having a rest, because nothing had ever been found. Cecilia thought her mother enjoyed holding court, having the hospital staff run around and listen to her amusing stories of concert halls and difficult conductors.

'What nonsense, Michael. You live in a modern flat with burglar alarms everywhere and a twenty-four hour caretaker. Anyway, it's insured, you needn't worry.'

I usually cleared my diary when Ana was in the Manor. I liked to be free to keep an eye on her as, despite all the adulation that surrounded her, she had a tendency to feeling low when reflecting on her health and (inevitably in such surroundings) her mortality. I also tried to find time to see my near neighbour, John Temple, who is quite frail, but totters across the corridor now and again to join me in a game of chess. Having been a senior partner with *Temple and Toms: fine violins, sales and valuations*, he had known a lot of musicians in his working life and enjoyed regaling me with anecdotes. Unfortunately, on this occasion he spotted the violin when I went to get the chess pieces from the cupboard.

'I didn't know you played.'

'I don't. I'm keeping it for a friend.'

He wandered across the room and stood beside me. 'Could I have a look?' He saw me hesitate and smiled. 'I did valuations for over thirty years.'

What else could I do but hand him the violin and pray he did not drop it. In the event, I became almost as uneasy as if he had damaged it, for after turning it over and over and weighing it, stroking it, plucking the strings and finally playing it, he handed it back with a look I couldn't read.

'I'm told it's a Gagliano,' I said eventually, wrapping it carefully in its silk cloth and replacing it in its case.

He gave a strange little laugh. 'So it says on the label.'

I poured him a glass of red wine. He sipped it and stared at the fire before setting it aside.

'What do you know about this violin?' he asked.

'It belongs to Ana Hirsch, that's all I know.' I wasn't going to repeat either her ridiculous story or Cecilia's equally unlikely childhood memories.

'Well, it's a fake. I wonder if her insurers know.'

We had two games of chess that night and I lost both. I

could not tell Ana what my neighbour had said, for of course it would mean admitting that I had let him handle her violin, something she never allowed anyone to do. In the end I grew tired of the whole affair. What was it to me if it had been rescued from a Polish village or bought in the Home Counties. Nor was it my problem if it was a fake.

It became my problem after Ana died, for she left it to me in her will.

As Cecilia stepped off the London train, I saw she was wearing the flimsy, but elegant, high heels I had admired the last time we met. Clearly she would not be able to walk even the short distance to the solicitor's office on High Street. I steered her towards the bus, wondering if I should mention that I could no longer afford taxis, now the season's recitals had been cancelled.

'Is this all right?'

Cecilia frowned. 'Don't confuse me with my mother. Buses were as foreign to her as taxis are to me.'

And before I could stop her she had bought our tickets and slipped into a seat behind a middle-aged woman who stood out from the other passengers, partly through her striking and rather foreign looks, partly from the superior, if not arrogant, way she looked around her. Cecilia gave me a nudge and nodded at her extravagant, elaborate hat. Then she gasped as she caught sight of the newly remodelled Frideswide Square.

'What's been going on here?'

'But you've been coming for weeks to see Ana.'

'By the Oxford Tube,' she said. 'I got on and off in Headington, there was no need to go into town.'

The rebuilding of the whole area around the Westgate Centre led to more sighs.

'It's unrecognisable! I had no idea this was going on. I suppose I've been in my own little bubble the last few months.'

I took her hand and she smiled up at me, her eyes brimming with tears.

The bus travelled up St Aldate's and we stood to move towards the door. She looked over my shoulder and whispered: 'At least you can always depend on Tom Tower.'

We stepped off the bus and stood for a moment looking back at the cream-coloured stone tower and archway, dominating its surroundings, before hurrying on to our appointment.

'Do you mind?' I asked Cecilia as we left the solicitor's office.

'I think it strange she left her violin to a pianist. I wish I understood why. But no, I don't mind. Of course not,' she said, slipping her arm into mine and leaning on me as we walked along High Street, towards the Covered Market. She had long ago lost that sulky look and had grown into a delightful person, even though, in my view, she had been ill-used by at least three lovers. And in recent years she had shown herself to be surprisingly tolerant of her mother's foibles, possibly because she was now well-known in her own right. We turned and walked through the market, stopping to buy bread, cheese, paté and finally fruit, as though we were preparing for a siege.

'There's something I forgot to tell you.' Cecilia slowed down and stopped me stepping out into the busy street. 'About the violin.'

'You do mind.'

'No, not at all. It's just something I found among my mother's things. A notebook my grandfather kept when he first arrived here. Difficult to read.'

'Impossible, I should have thought, unless you read Polish.'

'No, it was in English. He didn't know much and it was full of words and their meanings, a few idioms, the cost of food and travel and all sorts of scrappy bit and pieces. At the back he had written about his journey.'

'To practise his English?'

'Or because he wanted to remember. Anyway, he mentions the violin.'

'Really! So Ana hadn't made it up. Not the fantasist you accused her of being.'

Cecilia looked embarrassed. 'No, he really did escape bringing the violin all that way.' She paused a moment. 'But, of course, there's no way of knowing whether it was the Gagliano.'

Then we took the violin back to my place. We eventually finished eating and talking and now it was time. We played well into the night, choosing those pieces Ana had always avoided, wanting, I think, to establish something of our own. The music was no worse because the violin was a fake – if it really was. Nor did it matter any more whether it came from Poland in the war, or somewhere in Sussex or Surrey thirty years ago.

'I just wish she had left me a message,' I said.

'The Gagliano is the message,' Cecilia said with a smile.

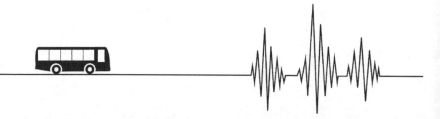

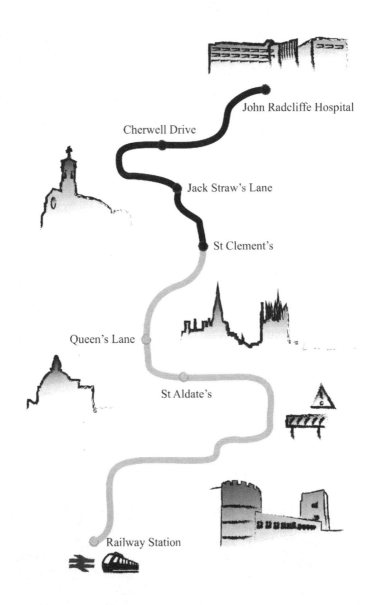

John Radcliffe Hospital

Cherwell Drive

Jack Straw's Lane

St Clement's

Queen's Lane

St Aldate's

Railway Station

Echoes

JANET BOLAM

A woman, white dress flowing, hat elegantly poised, is gliding through a garden of flowers. A man with a top hat walks at her side. The scene could be from a Monet painting, Le Dejeuner perhaps? Lizzy sees herself as they stroll down a gravel path. She notices the heat of the sun, the feel of the uneven path beneath her boots, and she yearns to reach out and touch the fine wool of the man's jacket, to compel him turn to kiss her.

Lizzy tried to recollect the particulars of her dream, its warp and weft, but the details drifted and dissolved. She felt she had lost something important. Harry was already up and in the bathroom. He emerged dressed, full of energy and purpose.

'Lizzy, you're awake. I didn't want to disturb you.' She noticed his overnight bag and document case stacked next to the door.

'Are you off already?'

'Yes, the conference starts at 9.15 sharp.'

'You mean you really had one?'

'Yes of course I have. I'm presenting to the Royal College of Surgeons. I told you.'

'I don't remember,' she faltered, 'and I filled in the breakfast thingy and hung it outside the door.'

'I don't eat breakfast.'

'I didn't know that! Never? You never eat breakfast?'

He shrugged, slightly embarrassed.

'Funny, isn't it?' she continued, as she pulled herself up 'we've known each other all this time. I suppose it's because we've never been with each other at breakfast time before.' Her comment hung between them like an accusation.

'Right. I'm off. I hope Leeds goes OK, and whatever you do, don't argue with your sister, and don't eat all the croissants or you'll get fat!' He leaned over the bed and gave her a peck on the cheek. 'I'll ring you when we're back in Oxford.'

Lizzy managed a nod and a smile. So, no leisurely breakfast together, after all? She picked up the TV remote and idly worked her way through the channels. The tap on the door made her start. Of course he's come back; how could he resist? She slipped on her silk dressing gown, quickly checked her hair in the ornate mirror, and composed her face.

'Your breakfast, Madam.' The waiter wheeled in a trolley, and with studied attention to detail, he spread a white cloth on the round table in front of the bay window, placed a small vase of flowers in the centre then carefully laid two places. 'Breakfast for two.' She considered the prettily set table, the romantic room and her disappointment. It was a genuine misunderstanding, she decided. After all, she hadn't actually asked him what he'd told his wife, she'd just assumed he'd make up an excuse so he could spend some time with her in London. Silly really, to get upset. She called Adele, her twin sister.

'Hi, I'll be a couple of hours early. Shall I meet you at the house?' They'd arranged to clear their mother's house, something they both dreaded and had put off, but now there really was no choice because it had been sold.

Three months ago, the terrible day their mother died, the sisters, reduced to a grief-stricken silence, mechanically cleared the house of food, stripped the beds, tidied up the worst of the chaos of books and clothes. Lizzy read the post-it notes that littered the walls above the old green telephone.

'I hadn't realized her memory was that bad!'

'Well you wouldn't would you? You were hardly ever here.' Adele had snapped.

'I live 200 miles away and you're just round the corner.'

'Harrogate is hardly just around the corner.'

'It's much nearer than Oxford.'

'So I got left to do everything.'

'I came up as much as I could, and if you remember correctly, I did come up after her surgery, and I had to take it out of my annual leave.'

'Which you resented doing at the time!'

'It just so happened to be an important week at work, but I moved heaven and earth to be here, and I was! We've been over this a hundred times, and Mum's hardly in her grave. So let's leave it for now! OK?'

Adele, a monument to misery, nodded. They gave each other a limp embrace, made a cup of tea and decided that they weren't ready to clear the whole house. Better to wait until they were strong enough, when they were less likely to beat each other up.

Their mother's house, the house they were brought up in, was a three bedroomed semi in Moortown, a 'leafy suburb' of Leeds. It was cold and damp, and now filled with the silence of desertion. Leaving Adele to pick up the mountain of junk mail, Lizzy moved from room to room. The kitchen hit her hard. It had once been warm and vibrant, where they shared chaotic mealtimes, friends and neighbours sitting across the formica kitchen table, mugs of tea in hand. She flicked through the Filofax that was always next to the telephone – *'If I lost that, I don't know where I'd be'* – then to the cupboard full of half tried homeopathic remedies, *'I know it's stupid, but it's worth a try.'* In the bedroom, she opened the wardrobe and the smell of patchouli oil caught her off guard. She pulled out a paisley patterned kaftan and pressed it to her face and only realized she was crying when great tears fell onto its worn cotton sleeve transforming the faded sage to a deep green. Half an hour later, Adele found her curled on the bed in a nest made of their mother's clothes.

'I brought Jaffa cakes' she sighed, 'just in case!' Lizzy hugged her and they sat side by side in silence.

Once they got going, it was easier than they thought. Soon there was a pile to throw away, a mountain of things to go to Oxfam and stacked on the dining table were items they wanted to keep. By early evening, they had finished the downstairs of the house, and were too exhausted to face the bedrooms or the contents of the loft, which had, in an earlier fit of enthusiasm, been heaved down onto the landing.

Paris 1892. She steps carefully out of a carriage into a cobbled courtyard. It's been raining and she's concerned not to wet the hem of her dress. A footman admits her to a large reception hall, where, with a big breath to control her nerves, she waits to be announced. She mounts a curved marble staircase that leads to a gathering of extravagant guests. The host turns from a circle of people and kisses her extended hand.

'Elizabeth!' he smiles. He doesn't remember inviting her, but his memory isn't as good as it was. 'I think you know everyone here,' he continues smoothly. 'We're just admiring a most marvelous new work by M. Monet. It's in the salon.' He indicates an adjoining room. As Elizabeth crosses the gold and green gilded room her eyes are searching and her smile is fixed. He isn't here! She breathes more easily, greets an acquaintance, allows herself to relax just a little. And then she sees him. The man with the top hat stands before a large easel at the far end of the room. Her heart springs then sinks as she sees that his wife is there next to him, hand placed proprietorially on his arm. She greets his wife warmly, gives her cheek a peck and engages in intense conversation, making sure she ignores her lover completely.

Lizzy lay on her back, tracing the lines of a crack that ran between the ceiling rose and the wall. It was 3.30 am. Closing her eyes, she allowed herself to experience the dream again. She could smell the street, the horse dung, raw grass, sewage, earth, and as she entered the expensive salon, heady with the scents of cloves and cinnamon.

Wide awake, she paced around trying to tire herself, and finally decided she might as well go through the boxes that had come down from the loft. She opened an octagonal hatbox decorated with bouquets of red and yellow flowers. It was crammed with manila envelopes, a pile of notebooks tied together with some lavender ribbon, some very old looking diaries and a large leather-bound photograph album. A glance at the diaries confirmed that the box had belonged to their mother's Aunt Sarah, an eccentric, rather glamorous divorcee who had a penchant for genealogy. Lizzie studied a photograph of her great grandparents at their wedding. She had seen a version of this before, elaborately framed, standing alongside a whole array of family photographs on the deep windowsill in her grandparents' front room. There was a date stamped in the corner. 1892. On the next page a large family group at the same wedding. She looked closely at the faces trying to imagine what their lives must have been like. A young woman, about the same age as her, was standing slightly apart from the group, fingers resting on a marble stand. For a wisp of a second, Lizzie could sense the marble, feel its cool smoothness. She had been there.

The room is blue and silver with a high ceiling, tall windows elegantly framed by silk curtains, the furniture classical. Propped against a chair are two simply framed paintings one of which has been attacked with an angry kick. Elizabeth tries to read, but feels too agitated to concentrate. A maid bobs in to tell her there's a visitor who insists on seeing her immediately. She pats her hair, stands on her tip-toes to see herself in the great gilded mirror that hangs above the fireplace. Then she seats herself, or rather poses, on the piano seat and begins to play a Chopin prelude. The man, top hat in hand, advances nervously towards her.

'Good morning' she manages an imperious tone, 'how kind of you to call on me.'

'Elizabeth, forgive me,' he begins. She returns to her Chopin as he notices the destroyed painting. He stares at her in disbelief as her playing becomes louder.

'Did you do this?' Elizabeth stops playing – a relief if truth be told – and faces him.

'You clearly prefer your precious paintings to me!'

'But this isn't just a painting. It's a work of genius!'

'Well it isn't any more, is it? For heaven's sake, just ask M. Monet for another one if you think it's so wonderful. I'm sure he can whip one up in a trice!' Like gladiators they lock eyes until the man relents.

'I lay awake all night . . .'

'Why would you lose one moment of sleep? After all, you were at a wonderful soirée with your beautiful, clearly devoted wife? Life surely cannot be happier for you?' She swept her arm in dramatic fashion. 'You lied to me and I can't forgive you. It was supposed to be our day together. Imagine my humiliation, waiting in a restaurant, alone? And then to be sent a cursory note to inform me of your regret at being unable to join me?'

*'My wife cancelled her trip to Deauville at the last moment. I
had no choice.'*
    'Really? '
    'I would have preferred to spend the evening with you'
    *'But you didn't.' She rises from the piano and flounces towards
the door. He catches her arm – as she no doubt intended – and
sweeps her into a deep, passionate kiss.*

'Rob let the twins watch Bambi yesterday, can you believe it?
They wouldn't go to sleep until I promised not to die. I need
strong tea,' Adele announced as she arrived the next morning.
They spent a long time looking through the photographs.

'I haven't seen this one before.' Adele picked out a bromide-
tinted photograph of two women, dressed almost identically,
in long culottes, blouses buttoned at their necks and straw hats
firmly on their heads. Two ungainly bicycles were propped on
a nearby tree. On the back of the photo, in a thin careful scroll,
it said Amelie and Elizabeth Servy, Bois de Boulogne, June
1891.

'Amelie was Mum's great grandmother which would make
her our great, great, grandmother.' Adele tapped her finger on
the picture. 'But do you remember anything about an
Elizabeth?'

'They must've been sisters. She must've been our great,
great aunt. Don't you think she looks like me?'

'Oh yes! I see what you mean. It's uncanny. Better dressed,
obviously.'

Leafing through a cluster of notebooks they found one entitled
'A Dark History'. Inside was Sarah's attempt at a family tree. A
mix of fact and personal comment, it was more a stream of
consciousness than an historical record. At the top of the page
she had written in her great looped scrawl 'Joseph and Anna
Servy arrive in Paris from the Ukraine 1863!!!' and beneath
that were the names and birth dates of their seven children,
among them, Amelie, born 1869 over which Sarah had written
'My Grandmother, May Her Soul Rest in Peace'. 'Elizabeth
b1871' was circled boldly, 'My glamorous Aunt. A friend of

Joseph + Anne Serninski
uurie in Poris from the
Ukraine 1863!!!

My grandmother
Way her soul
Rest in Peace

Joseph Serninski
m 1857
Anna Markowicz

Arthur
b. 1859

Estelle
b. 1861
d. 1861

Rachel
b. 1861

Louis
b. 1863

Charlie
b. 1865

Amelie
b. 1869

Elizabeth
b. 1871

My glamorous
Aunt. Afraid of
Monet, Manet, Renoir
and Cezanne!

? ? ? ? ?

Rachel
b. 1892

Claude
b. 1917

Frederick
b. 1917

Amelia
b. 1920

Sarah
b. 1926

Bernard
b. 1946

Julia
b. 1949

Adele
b. 1985

Elizabeth
b. 1985

Manet, Monet, Renoir and Cezanne!' Underneath her name, there was an embellished question mark.

'I wish we'd asked about this sort of thing when we could. We have a direct connection to Manet, Monet, Renoir!' sighed Lizzy wistfully.

'Oh you know Aunt Sarah was as mad as a box of frogs. She probably made most of it up.'

'Still, I bet she knew all about great, great Aunt Elizabeth.'

'So, Lizzy, how's things? How's the new job going?' Rob had mellowed now the children were asleep, and the remains of lasagna and two bottles of red wine surrounded them.

'Absolutely fabulous. Couldn't be better.'

'And are you still seeing the lovely Harry-the-knife?'

'How did you know I was seeing him? Did Adele tell you?' Lizzy looked accusingly at her sister.

'Well you know how I feel about it' said Adele who had drunk most of a bottle of Rioja.

'Yes, you've been very clear on the subject.'

'I'd kill Rob if he did it to me. Did you hear that Rob? I'd kill you. Tell me something,' she leaned forward, her voice slightly slurring, 'why hasn't he left his wife to live with you yet?'

'I've never asked him to.'

'But don't you want him to?'

'Not particularly. I'm happy with things as they are.'

'Are you really?'

'Yes, why wouldn't I be?'

'Because you've been seeing him for months and months!'

'So?'

'You must like him a lot more than you let on. Otherwise, why are you wasting your time?'

'Adele, you've had too much to drink,' Rob intervened. 'Let's change the subject.'

'I don't want to change the subject!'

'I'm sorry, Lizzy, she's very drunk.'

'Don't you make excuses for me,' Adele waved a fork in Rob's direction, 'what I'm saying is true, and we all know it!'

'And what are you saying, precisely?' asked Lizzy in a crisp voice.

Adele hesitated for a few moments before she levelled,

'What's happening to you? Who are you trying to kid when you say stupid things like "I don't want him to leave his wife. I'm happy as things are?" Because the only fool is you.'

'Is this another example of Miss-oh-so-perfect, you telling me what a failure I am?'

'Stop making this about something else. All I'm saying is it breaks my heart to see you throwing yourself away on a married man.'

'Who says I'm throwing myself away?'

'If he ever intended to leave his wife for you, he would've done it by now.'

'Like you'd know! That's your trouble Adele. You always think you know better than me about my life! You don't and I wish you'd stop all this "holier than thou" crap you throw at me. I'm off to bed.'

They stood on a Japanese Bridge that curved over a lake abundant with pink lilies. Elizabeth is proudly wearing her new dress, white with small dark blue spots, and a red sash beaded with flowers tied around her waist. She's pleased with the matching hat because it goes well with her hair. Claude wants to photograph the water lilies in his garden at Giverny and he has persuaded Elizabeth and the man with the top hat to pose. Elizabeth's face hurts from the smile she has to hold throughout the long exposure, her feet ache and the feeling of nausea she's been experiencing on-and-off for a while now, has returned with a vengeance. A thin bead of sweat courses down the face of the man in the top hat.

'Fini.' Claude declared himself delighted with his efforts and hurried off with the plates to the dark room.

'Thank goodness that's over,' Elizabeth swept off her hat and used it as a fan. 'I think the others are in the orchard. Let's go.' She set off, and after a moment's delay, the man with the top hat followed.

The next morning they worked hard, but in silence. Adele felt guilty for upsetting Lizzy as much as she had.

'I know. Why don't we take a few hours off and go to the

Monet exhibition?' she suggested. Lizzie acknowledged the proffered olive branch with relief.

'Are you sure? You hate Monet.'

'But you love him. I'll give him one more chance.'

The gallery was full of people slowly shuffling past a series of elaborately mounted paintings. There was a logjam around the water lilies, and no one seemed to notice a small painting of a young woman standing alone on a hill, the wind tugging at her white dress and parasol. Lizzie's heart beat so fast it hurt, her mouth felt dry and her legs nearly gave from under her. She had dreamt this. Exactly this.

'What are the chances of a false-positive?' Lizzy asked herself, as she drove back to Oxford. But she had known, even before she saw the telltale blue line of the pregnancy testing kit. Nothing in her life felt stable anymore; her mother's death, moving flats, Harry, the dreams and now this. She had a splitting headache and her shoulders were hunched with tension. Pulling into Trowell Services, she downed some Nurofen with strong black coffee and tried to relax. The drunken conversation with Adele cycled through her mind and she knew she had no choice but to sort things out with Harry.

'Can I see you tomorrow?' she texted him.

He replied quickly.

'Yes.'

'Fancy a walk in Shotover?'

'I've got a clinic in the afternoon, so sixish?'

It felt like they had the place to themselves. They sat in a small glade enjoying the late sun. They could see the BMW factory and the rooftops around Cowley and on a hill over the valley, the great white buildings of the John Radcliffe hospital.

'Just think,' Lizzy tucked her arm through his and leaned on his shoulder, 'people have looked over these hills since the Stone Age.'

'Good vantage point. You can see all your enemies coming.'

'I suppose so.'

'Do you know what the advantage of this is for this particular Early Man? Me see no one else here! Me see my beautiful Lizzy and me want to make love to her!' He thumped his chest with his free hand in mock stone age style. She laughed and kissed him.

'I've been thinking,' she began gently, 'how would you feel about us becoming something a bit more permanent?' she had practised this many times, but it still felt stilted when she finally heard herself say it.

'What do you mean?' Lizzy felt his shoulder tense.

'We've been together now for nearly a year, and I just think we should be a bit braver.'

'You really have been doing some thinking. But why now?'

'Because I've been thinking about the future, and us, that sort of thing.'

'It's been tough for you these last weeks, but I thought you were . . . OK with how things are between us.'

'I was, I am. But things change, don't they? They have for me, at least.'

'What do you mean?'

'I'm pregnant.' She looked at Harry willing him to be pleased.

'This is all a bit sudden,' he managed. Lizzy could hear his heartbeat rise.

'I'm just as upset as you are,' Lizzy sat up to face him, 'but we've been seeing each other for over a year. This isn't ideal, but –' she petered out.

Harry was silent for a long time.

'I don't think you realize how complicated it is for me. Mandy and Jonny are the most important people in my life – I've never hidden that from you.'

'I know,' Lizzy cut in 'I do know how important they are to you, but we could work something out. I thought perhaps Mandy and Jonny could come to live with us?'

'Live with us?' Harry's look chilled her. All his warmth had drained, replaced with an unmistakable look of fear. This was going terribly wrong.

'You've told me that hundreds of times you and Linda aren't happy together. I just assumed . . .'

'I've never said I'd leave her Lizzy. I've never said that.'
Harry tried to be gentle

'But you aren't happy, are you?'

'Linda's the mother of my children and that counts for something.'

'I'll be the mother of your child. Doesn't that count for something too? '

'So you're going to have it?'

'What? Of course. What do you mean?'

'And is it ?'

'Oh my God! Yes, it is yours!'

The wind gave a sudden gust making the leaves rustle. There was the distant sound of a woman calling for her dog.

'I'm not proud of myself.'

'Because you're ashamed of me?' her voice began to shake.

'No, not of you! But of what I'm doing, yes, I'm ashamed! '

'And here was me thinking it was just a matter of time before – before –' she broke down in tears. He leaned towards her to try to comfort her, but she shook him off. She worked hard to control herself before she said 'I'm such a fool. Drive me home please.'

Elizabeth is sitting on a green ironwork bench in the Parc Monceau. The man in the top hat joins her. She is weeping. He tells her he will look after her, that she and the baby will want for nothing. He wipes away her tears.

Yesterday's humiliation lurked like an unwelcome guest, a bad taste in Lizzy's mouth. It took a few days before she could bear to think about her situation with more detachment. What had she expected?

Honfleur. Elizabeth and the man with the top hat eat fish and drink the local wine in a café next to the harbor. The smell of the sea air, salt, tar, coal dust. Someone starts to play an accordion and almost immediately, there is gusty singing that moves from crowded café to crowded café. Elizabeth wants to join in; she is, after all, on holiday, on the way to London. The man with the top hat is distracted and silent as he pays the bill and they go back to their hotel.

At the port the following day, there is talk of a storm, but the boat sails anyway. The sea is rough and the violent churning of the boat makes Elizabeth feel sick. The man with the top hat insists she climb up to the deck to get some fresh air. The deck is deserted. Suddenly, he pins her against the rail. At first she thinks he wants to keep her secure against the rocking of the boat. The sea was so wild the spray hits her face, drenches her clothes.

'Lets go back in, I'm soaked' she shouts against the roar of the storm. But still he pins her to the rail. She tries to move.

'Let me go!' But instead he grips around her waist and with a sudden heave, starts to force her over the rail. She twists and shouts, beats at his head. His eyes are vacant, his face screwed to the effort. She screams but the sea and the wind drown any sound.

The shock, the struggle, the fall, the hard smack of the ice-cold sea, the heavy drag of her dress. Down and down. Lizzy screamed into wakefulness, fighting, taking huge gulps of air. Vivid, searing, she relived this nightmare by night and it consumed her by day.

When Harry finally phoned, he invited her to meet him for lunch at the hospital. Clever of him to ask to meet her at his workplace – she was hardly likely to create a scene in the middle of the hospital canteen. She felt too dizzy, too short of sleep to drive so she began to walk through town, but by the time she reached the Plain she was tired. She was relieved to find a bus stop outside the Thai restaurant that went all the way to the hospital. As she sank down into her seat a sharp flash of red caught her eye. The man she was sitting next to was trying to hide a gaudy red book down the side of the seat. Probably porn, she concluded because she could almost touch the feeling of guilt flowing from him. She looked around, trying to decide if she could discreetly move seats, but the bus was moving again. He slowly drew the book onto his lap and began reading, careful to hide the cover. Lizzie strained her eyes until they hurt; she was curious to know what he was reading, but all she could make out was that it was hand-written. Probably not porn then. The bus lurched and so did Lizzy's stomach. The morning nausea was developing into an all day event.

Harry met her in the League of Friends Café. She was sure this meeting was going to be difficult so when he greeted her with a smile and a hug she was surprised. He suggested they went to the sensory garden, a small quiet corner in the hospital grounds.

'It was the shock,' Harry explained. 'I didn't mean what I said. I needed time to think. I want to look after you, and the baby. I want to. Don't worry, we'll find a way.' He leaned into Lizzy and wiped away her tears. He led her towards a small bench. She noticed the heat of the sun on her back, the feel of the uneven path under her feet. She yearned to touch his arm, to compel him to kiss her. She still loved him.

'I thought we might steal a weekend away together?' he murmured, 'I thought perhaps Honfleur?'

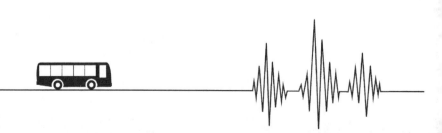

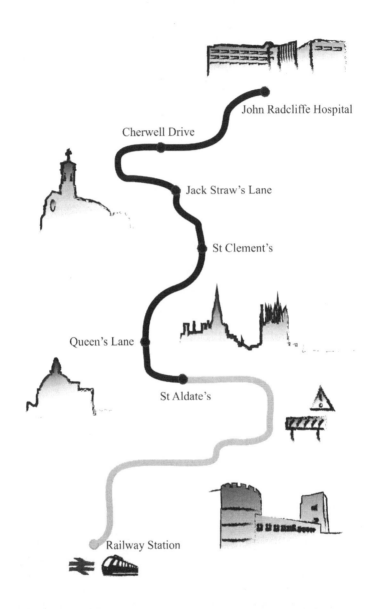

John Radcliffe Hospital

Cherwell Drive

Jack Straw's Lane

St Clement's

Queen's Lane

St Aldate's

Railway Station

The Journal

GRAHAM BIRD

On the bus

The notebook slid under my feet when the bus shuddered to a halt. We had reached St Clement's and an old woman had stepped onto the crossing without warning.

'Sorry everybody,' the driver shouted back to us all.

Polite, I thought. I picked it up and turned it over. The cover was a coral fabric with gold, silver and blue beaded decorations. A length of orange wool secured the contents. I hesitated. Had anyone else noticed? Probably not, the two women at the front were busy arguing and the lady sniffing and rummaging in her handbag looked to be in her own little world.

Another late shift awaited, not my favourite because the afternoon seemed to bring out the worst in people. Patients who were hungry, visitors who would not keep their voices down. I clutched my prize and looked around again to be certain no-one saw. Someone must have dropped this. I untied the woollen cord and lifted the front cover. On the first page was a handwritten note.

If you find this journal, I must have lost it. Please be kind and call me on 07788 123456. I'm Maggie, by the way. Thanks!

She had put tiny stickers of smiley faces all around the note and I conjured up a picture of Maggie: a bohemian artist, nineteen and studying art at Oxford Brookes. I put the journal in my shoulder-bag. It would be too embarrassing to call her while on the bus so I looked out the window and watched two mothers walking with buggies towards the park, chatting as their babies slept. I took the journal out again and ran my fingers over the cover. Could I resist? Perhaps I could find out more about arty Maggie. Perhaps she made the cover.

I paused, then gave in and opened it. There were a few pages of writing, a couple of photos, followed by more writing that was a neat, spidery flow in green ink. Each page was a different day, and it looked like she had been keeping this journal since the beginning of the year. I read the first page.

Day one of not smoking. Simon says I mustn't (and he should know!). A difficult day back at work, tried to keep busy. Perhaps I should get a new job, I deserve more, but then there's Simon to consider. Janey phoned and told me all about her Christmas with the parents. I thought mine were bad.

I flicked through a few more pages then looked at the photos. They were taken in a booth and she was laughing while he pulled a serious face. In the second photo he was kissing her cheek, and it looked like she was sitting on his knee. I knew him.

I shut the journal with a slam and re-wrapped the cord. My heart was thumping. Someone would notice me. I put it back in my bag and sat, staring out the window at the passing streets.

Mr Simon Brownley. Trauma Surgeon. A man with a steady hand. I had worked with him, not regularly but I had seen him on the ward, even stood beside him while he spoke to a man called George who had broken both legs under a mangled motor-bike. George was my patient and I walked with him every day for three weeks until he was discharged. I had seen Simon Brownley's handiwork at first hand.

My dream of a gorgeous hippy student evaporated as I realised the woman in the pictures must be Maggie. She looked about my age, pretty face, dark hair, and happy. She looked single, I thought, not that I could tell. Mr Simon Brownley, with a wife and the two teenage children who I met in the garden of the White Horse last summer, was definitely not single.

Still, that's hospitals for you, who was I to judge?

We turned left past the Co-op in Old Marston, then right into Cherwell Drive, back towards the JR, before we stopped outside the main doors. I slung my bag over my shoulder and made my way to the locker rooms to change. I hated commuting in my uniform as I got fed up with school-kids joking with me about being a nurse. Alison, my boss, was ready to hand over.

'We're full to bursting. A&E are putting on the pressure today,' she said.

The afternoon went fast. Three hours before a break and it was almost six o'clock before I had chance to think about Maggie. I took a moment to search the hospital contact database. There were two Maggies and one of those was in the Churchill so she couldn't possibly be on my 13 bus. It had to be Maggie Foster, executive assistant to the Director of IT.

I hesitated. In that moment, my pager beeped and I went to find Alison. The lovely Maggie would have to wait.

The next day

It was 10 p.m. when I finished and too late to phone her. I read the journal all the way home on the bus. I couldn't help myself. It started with an entry for every day, but by March it was thinning out and when I got to June there was only one jotting a week. The most recent said:

I'm living the dream. Career on the up, and Simon says he loves me. Does that mean he does? I guess so . . . Simon says.

I decided I would lie if she asked whether I had looked at it. Maybe she wouldn't ask anyway – too embarrassed. I should give it back tomorrow.

Waking at nine o'clock the next morning, I put in the washing and fetched milk and bread. I shared the flat with three other men, so it was always a complete tip, not somewhere I could bring a girl back. Fat chance anyway, no time for dating. I had met a few girls through 'Match' but nothing lasted more than a couple of weeks, mostly ruined by my shift patterns. Lucy was the only one I really liked, she worked in an accounts office in town and we saw each other occasionally for cinema or coffee dates. 'There's plenty of time,' my mother would say when I phoned her on a Friday morning.

I left the flat to go to the Costa on Magdalen Street and rang the phone number on the way. Just outside the Randolph, there were a few spots of rain in the air and a man was unloading luggage and wedding suits from the boot of a grey

Mercedes. I stood and watched him, presumably the groom, as he discussed the weather with the concierge on the steps. Oxford was already busy for the summer and the hotel lobby area was full of Japanese tourists.

'Hello, is that Maggie?' I held the phone close and protected the mouthpiece from the breeze.

'Yes, who is that?' She sounded cool, smooth and professional. The image of her smile filled my mind.

'It's Ben. Ben Curtis. I'm a nurse on the trauma ward.'

'Oh, ok. How can I help? Are the phones down?'

'No, no, nothing like that. I'm not at work at the moment, but I got your mobile number from . . .'

'Ben Curtis, did you say?' She interrupted.

'. . . Yes, that's right.'

I could hear tapping in the background.

'Oh, I see you, yes, Staff Nurse Curtis, a bank nurse. What do you want, Ben?'

I hesitated. She was feisty. Already. I pulled my coat around me and faced the wall of the Randolph to block out the people passing, and the traffic noise. I should have waited until I was somewhere quieter.

'It's just that I . . . well, I catch the 13 bus to work. I did yesterday afternoon.'

This time she was the one who paused. I could hear her cough and then she whispered.

'Did you see me on the bus? I get that one. From the station.'

'Oh no, well I . . . yes. I get on at St Aldate's. But I didn't see you. I'm working lates this week. I, um . . .'

Just then a coach started reversing right beside me, its beeping drowning out her voice. I carried on walking towards the corner and turned right, opposite the Martyrs' Memorial. Its stonework was a grimy yellow and the surrounding steps were filled with a group of visiting school-kids, no doubt learning about the three protestant martyrs who were burned at the stake. A smell of fresh ciabatta drifted out of the deli behind me.

'So why are you calling me?' She said.

'I have your journal. It was on the bus yesterday.'

I heard a slight gasp and I waited for her to answer.

'That's amazing, Ben. Thank you so much. I can't thank you enough. Oh, my God. I had no idea where I had left it.'

'It must have lodged under the back seat because it slid by my feet when the bus stopped.'

'Are you in work today?' she said.

'Yes, this afternoon. I have a break about five.'

'I could call by your ward.'

'No. Don't do that. Let's meet in the café, the one on the third floor.'

'Ok, that's fine. I finish around then anyway, so I'll see you in there. Thank you so much.'

'Great – see you then.'

'How will you know me?'

'Oh, um . . . well, I . . . I saw your photo.' I said, then regretted it. I hadn't thought this lie through. What exactly had I read?

'Oh yes, I understand. I will see you by the cold drinks machine. Thanks Ben.'

I walked on to Costas and ordered an Americano, then sat and stared at the passers-by. What would I say to her? She was making a big mistake, but it was nothing to do with me. I texted Lucy.

Fancy a movie night on Saturday? Ben X

Two minutes later, I was abandoned again.

At a friend's hen weekend. Sorry.

Not even a kiss or 'Perhaps another time.' I banged the table so hard the coffee spilled into the saucer.

The coffee

The JR coffee was strong, black and my favourite. An acquired taste. Maggie had tea and we sat facing each other, in the corner furthest from the vending machines. The café served twenty-four hours a day but its busiest times were in the morning. By five o'clock the place was down to a few visitors waiting for news of loved ones, or the occasional staff member on a late break.

'Thanks for this, I could have picked it up from you,' she said.

I smiled my best smile and picked up my coffee.

'You're welcome. It's no trouble.'

Maggie's beautiful face was even better than in her photo. She had hazel eyes, shoulder-length wavy dark hair tucked back behind tiny ears with diamond stud earrings. She looked tidy, organised and business-like. Her jacket was navy-blue covering a white blouse, and she wore a blue skirt just above the knee. Perfect legs, though I hardly dared sneak a look.

I pulled the journal from my pocket and handed it across the table. She glanced at it before pushing it into the depths of her bright orange handbag.

'So you found my number in the front?'

'Yes and, look, I have to be honest.'

I had practised this line all morning. She stared at me until I carried on.

'I looked inside. I read a few pages until I realised it was a personal journal.' She grinned as I squirmed.

'You know about Simon, then.'

'Mr Brownley. Yes. I saw. I know him,' I said.

'Look, please. It's not what you think. I'm embarrassed you saw it, but it will all come out soon anyway. Please keep it to yourself.'

She picked up her tea and finished it as if she was about to leave. I wanted to agree with her, she looked so confident, but I knew it was a mistake, she was too good for him. I had dealt with headstrong patients before, they need time to talk, to see reason. My delaying tactic was to take another sip of coffee, my mug half full.

'I love this coffee,' I said.

'Simon says it's the best in the hospital.'

'Please be careful. You know he has a family,' I said.

'Yes. It's tricky. But it is what it is. And not your business,' she said.

I hesitated.

'I mean. Thank you for the journal. I'm sure you're a wonderful person, but it's my life. Mine and Simon's,' she said.

'You know he's much older. Has a reputation. Previous affairs.'

She stood and glowered. Fiery. She slung her bag over her shoulder.

'Please be circumspect with what you know. His medical reputation is second-to-none. He's brilliant.'

I took another sip and looked up at her. Her heels added to her height, her strength.

'I'm not worried about his reputation. I'm concerned about you. I implore you to think, to be careful, that's all. You seem like a good person, young and very attractive. Please, I'm not trying to interfere. I cannot un-know what I know.'

Her face went a little redder, and she smiled at me, then sighed.

'Ben, it's decided. We're in love. I'll be fine. Is it a reward you require?'

I put on a shocked face and laughed. I realised I had nothing more to say. It wasn't like she was my girlfriend, much as I might wish it.

'Just think about what you're doing. That's all. Think of me as your sensible friend, your voice of reason.'

I finished my coffee as she turned and walked away. I'd like to see her again, I thought.

The Weekend

That should have been the end of it, of course. I should have let it go. I couldn't get her out of my head all weekend, my first off in four weeks. Lucy bombed me out and the guys in the flat were at a nightclub I couldn't afford. Saturday night in watching Casualty . . . ironic but I loved it. Doctors chasing nurses, directors bedding assistants, life was one long soap opera. Maggie needed a knight in shining armour.

I sent her a text-message on Sunday morning. I felt bold though not bold enough to call.

Hi Maggie, Would you like to meet me for a beer one evening? I'm on early shift all week, Regards Ben (the one who found your journal)

I looked at it, then deleted it. Too formal. I started again.

*Hiya Maggie, Fancy a beer one evening? I'm on earlies this week.
Ben x*

I struck out the x and then pressed send.

I went down the pub for lunch, my local served the best roast beef, an indulgence for a Sunday off. She replied after a couple of hours.

If I must. Whatever it takes. Tonight. King's Arms in town. 7:30.

Crikey. I needed a shower and a change.

I got there early and stood at the bar. The pub was buzzing with students and people enjoying a sunny evening in June. A group of Korean students took up the Wadham room, having a celebratory party for the completion of their course. The King's Arms was the height of elegance in Victorian days, an inn for anyone who couldn't afford the Randolph. Nowadays it had turned into a well-stocked ale house with a lively atmosphere.

I ordered a cider and waited. Maggie arrived fifteen minutes late with no apology. I bought her a white wine and luckily we found seats at the end of a bench table where we could talk privately. She looked divine in a flowery top and tight jeans with those same black heels.

'You want to have another go at me, I assume,' she said.

I came from a different angle. Perhaps we could be friends.

'I love working at the JR. Most of the time. It can be very rewarding. How about you? How's life in IT?'

'I saw Simon last night, you know.'

'He's an excellent surgeon. I admire him. There are some very good people at the hospital. I trained in London, UCH, and I moved here over three years ago. I'm from Oxford.'

'I went to uni in London, then I went travelling,' she said.

We drank slowly and chatted easily. The ambience of the place lent itself to friendship and she started to mellow. She had drifted into her job through a friend of an old boyfriend. She was good with spreadsheets and numbers. She liked Madonna and The Black Eyed Peas. She thought Beyoncé and Emma Thompson were strong female role models and she preferred beer to cider. She'd been to Glastonbury in the rain and walked the beaches of Koh Samui. We had another, then another.

'Ben, you must let it go, you know. Simon and I are for keeps,' she said.

'I really like you. That's all. I feel I know you. Will I appear in your journal for today?'

She laughed and said she should be going. It was like she was toying with me so I got angry.

'Don't ruin your life with him. Be with me instead.' I blurted out.

She glared.

'You have to give him up,' I said.

'And how do you propose to make me?'

'I'll tell him all about your journal. I'll tell him about us. I'll tell him this affair will be broadcast to the world.'

'Don't be daft. I've already told him I lost it and you've kindly recovered it. No damage done. His wife has probably guessed anyway. There's really nothing you can do to harm us.'

On the way home, I texted her.

Sorry, I overstepped the mark. It's just that I like you very much. Take care. Have a good life, Ben x

This time I didn't strike out the x.

Monday

I tried to catch the same bus as her on Monday morning, even though I was on a late. I knew she started at nine but she said she was often early. I checked the number 13 timetable and hurried to my St Aldate's stop for just after eight. She wasn't on the first bus that passed so I waited for the next. By the time the third one came, I gave up and boarded anyway.

As we went over the Magdalen Bridge, I got a text and pulled my phone out, hoping it would be her.

Ben, please come and see me as soon as you get in today. Alison

Strange, I always reported to Alison when I arrived anyway. Why would she send that? It ruined the rest of the journey. Had I made a mistake, administered the wrong drug, attended the wrong patient, filled in the wrong form? A nurse's life was like a high-wire act, so easy to slip.

I stood up as we went up Saxon Way to make sure I got off first, and as soon as we pulled in, I rushed through the corridors to her office.

'Come in Ben. Take a seat,' she said.

Already she seemed formal.

Before I could speak, she turned over the papers on her desk and I could read my name at the top.

'The thing is Ben, I'll get straight to it. We're facing more cuts and your name is at the top of my list. I can't book you in for any more shifts. I'm sorry, I can write a good reference.'

'You're sacking me?' I said.

'Of course not, we're just letting you go. You're not permanent, you're a bank nurse.'

I could hardly speak, determined not to crack.

'But I've been here a while now. Longer than most.'

She shifted in her seat and fiddled with her pen, avoiding my look as she stared at the paperwork.

'Why me?'

'Well, I suppose you deserve a straight answer. There's been a complaint.'

Somehow I knew. I didn't need to ask.

Going home

I walked out of the office, straight back to the bus-stop. I was too upset to clear my locker and say good-bye to people. Too angry, too shocked. I would come back tomorrow. Alison was fine with that.

A woman sat in my favourite seat with a boy beside her who looked about ten and very pale. Probably been seen by him, I thought.

I squeezed past and sat in the back, putting on my head-phones. When I got off, I walked through Cornmarket past the shops. I called her and she didn't answer so I left a message.

You two have had my contract cancelled. He's a bastard and you should be ashamed. I'm a good nurse.

Somehow that wasn't enough. I couldn't leave it like that. I turned around and went back to the High Street, and walked down to the Queen's Lane stop. I would get my money's worth from the season ticket today. My redundant season ticket. The bus seemed to take an age to return to the JR and I almost got off at every stop. When we arrived, I thanked the driver.

'Here goes nothing,' I said.

He looked at me strangely and wished me luck. He could never guess why.

This time I walked different corridors, went up in the lift and strode with purpose to his office. The door was shut but there was a glass panel and I could see him sitting there, typing some piece of poison no doubt. I didn't knock. He stood up with a start.

'Can I help?' he said.

I walked over and swung my fist, landing it on his chin before he even had time to raise his arm. I had never hit a person in my twenty-eight years. There went my career. I didn't care. He reeled back as if he was in a cartoon movie and came back upright. I swung again and missed.

'What the . . .' he shouted, then tried to shove me back.

'Leave Maggie alone,' I shouted before turning away. My work was done, my knuckles stung.

'Don't bother calling the police. Not unless you want this all over the *Oxford Mail*,' I said.

I walked out and shut the door behind me.

At the bus-stop, the 13 would be another ten minutes. I was tempted to walk. What if he came after me? My whole body was shaking and my wrist was sore.

I sent one final text to Maggie.

If you ever want to talk, call me. Ben xx

When the bus arrived, it was the same driver as the one in the morning.

'Had a good day, nurse? You people do wonderful work.' he said.

'Oh, the best of days, thanks. I should start a journal.'

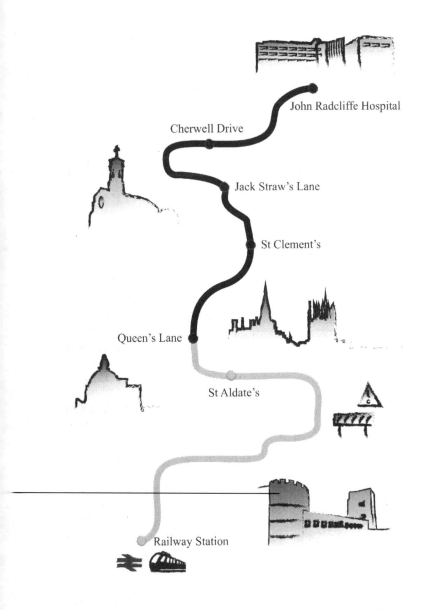

John Radcliffe Hospital

Cherwell Drive

Jack Straw's Lane

St Clement's

Queen's Lane

St Aldate's

Railway Station

No Left Turn

ANNIE WINNER

The meeting had been dragging on for what seemed like hours and as always Frances tried, and failed, to contain her impatience.

'Can't we leave that one till next time?' she said brusquely, tapping the table-top with her pen.

David, the chair of the meeting, had lost the thread of the argument going on round the table, and grasped this opportunity with relief.

'Good idea, Frances,' he said. 'Deferred until the next meeting. Let's move on to item 7 on the agenda. Colin – you were going to lead off on this.'

Frances was soon in a bog of boredom again and distracted herself by making a mental list of what she had to get through by the time she had to leave to pick the kids up at 2.30 p.m., occasionally making a contribution and once again wondering why she had to be here. Her distraction was interrupted by the buzzing of her mobile, set to 'Silent and Vibrate'. Saved! she thought as she mouthed 'Sorry – I've got to take this' at David and released herself into the corridor. It was her mother.

'It's your Dad. He had a funny turn at breakfast this morning and they've taken him into the John Radcliffe. We're there now.'

Frances felt the usual mixture of exasperation and alarm that her mother's increasingly frequent over-dramatic calls triggered. Until now none of them had materialised into anything serious, but she knew that one day one would. The last time she'd had a call from her mother from their local hospital, she'd dropped everything and belted up the motorway to Nottingham only to find that her father had cut his finger on a garden knife.

She momentarily thought, 'What were they doing in Oxford?' Then she remembered that her parents had been visiting one of her father's old friends who lived in a village a few miles south of the city.

'All right Mum, I'll come as fast as I can.' She hurried down the corridor to her office. Sue, her secretary, looked up from her screen.

'What's up?'

Frances explained, and, thinking fast, asked Sue to cancel her diary for today. She phoned Toby – it went straight to voicemail, and then her friend and neighbour Linda to ask her to collect the kids if Toby didn't make it. Only half an hour later she was on the train hurtling south across the green textures of North Oxfordshire.

Although they lived in Banbury she seldom went back to Oxford, but she did remember that there was a direct bus from the station to the hospital, and sure enough, as she emerged into the station forecourt a number 13 drew in and the waiting queue started to board. Frances clambered her way to the back, tucking herself into the corner seat as the bus bumped its way past the Said Business School to the traffic lights. She sat back in her seat and drifted into the musing mode often launched by bus journeys. Inevitably she was reminded of the years she had lived in Oxford as the bus passed various reminders of her earlier life. She looked to her right as it passed the entrance to Christchurch Meadow where she and Richard had often walked on summer evenings.

When the bus stopped outside the Town Hall, tantalisingly incomplete images of those times floated through her mind's eye. On an impulse she decided to get off the bus. As she walked up towards Cornmarket Street she thought she caught a fleeting glimpse of the barman she had often chatted with when they drank at the Bear. It couldn't be him, she knew, but that glimpse enabled her to begin to contemplate her memories with a degree of calm.

She turned into the High Street and went into the Covered Market. She remembered several of the shops and stalls – the florist, the cheese stall, the Hat Box – but there were a number of new outlets too. The café where they had often gone for a coffee in their lunch hour was still there, although it had been smartened up. She had always loved the feel and smells of the

Covered Market and she was tempted to stop for a coffee, but then she remembered the urgency in her mother's voice and went back out into the High Street. She walked down past the glowing stone facades searching the bus stop signs for the 13, finding it outside the Queen's College. She glanced down to the Queen's Lane Coffee House, another haunt in her former life. She knew that she was stalling when once again she had to resist the longing for a coffee as she waited for the next bus. It soon rolled up and she again went to the seat at the back on the left, vaguely noting a rather tearful looking woman with hair dyed a sizzling red sitting near the front and another in a lurid green dress. She could feel the lid she had kept on what happened that day slipping open as the bus rolled down the High Street.

She caught a glimpse of the traffic turning up into Longwall Street and saw the trees in Magdalen College. This time she couldn't bat away the flood of images. She was back on that pavement, feeling the grit on her bare knees as she knelt over the inert body, hearing a disembodied voice screaming 'Richard! Richard!' They had been free-wheeling on their bikes down the High Street, then waiting at the lights at the bottom, Richard ahead. They were on their way back to her flat in the Cowley Road, and as the lights changed he'd set off to go straight on but the lorry on their right had suddenly turned left without indicating.

The horror of that day was dredged up in jerky snapshots; the blood pouring from his head, the wail of the ambulance siren, the passing strangers ineptly trying to console her, the crumpled ruin of his bike, the defensive blustering of the lorry driver. She drew a deep breath and tried to steady herself, realising that for all she'd suffered over the following years, the pain of that moment was barely tempered.

Richard had not died, but the impact of his head injuries had often made her wish he had. He'd been in hospital for months and then in rehab at Stoke Mandeville for even longer. He was no longer the funny, clever, sensitive, passionate man she'd loved so dearly, but could barely get his mouth around a word, despite the best efforts of the speech therapists. He was doubly incontinent, unable to walk and sometimes she felt he barely knew who she was. After a few months she started to wonder why she carried on slogging up to Aylesbury on the bus and then on another one out to Stoke Mandeville twice a week to visit him.

For months, Frances agonised, weighing the rights and wrongs of the bind she was in. She would wake with a start in the middle of the night and her mind would start churning over her dilemma. She would half doze off, then wake again – often from a dream of a vibrant, laughing, loving Richard, but seconds later be plunged into the pit again. She would make her mind up – she could not go on being his saintly girlfriend, and at her next visit she would tell him. Then she would see him, and his eyes would seem to light up when she entered his room – and she would be disarmed again. She felt too guilty and ashamed to talk to anyone about it as the warmth of her love for Richard diminished in surges over the long months, and feelings of resentment started to be added to the cocktail of grief and guilt.

Frances had only met Richard's parents once before the accident. They lived in Manchester and did not drive, so visiting was even more difficult for them. They seemed wary of her, and somehow managed to make her feel at least partially responsible for the accident, implying that if he hadn't been going to her flat it wouldn't have happened. Although she'd tried to keep in touch, ringing them regularly, she never felt they welcomed her efforts and they never rang her. Eventually they had all been invited to a meeting with Richard's doctor at which he rather brutally told them that little or no further improvement could be expected, and arrangements needed to be made for his future care.

'I'm really sorry,' she'd cried, through choking sobs, 'but I can't do this any more'. She had stumbled out of the room and fled down the corridor, out into the sunlight, out into her future – without him.

By now some of the other passengers were casting veiled glances at Frances as she sniffed loudly and rummaged in her bag for a tissue. A rather scruffy-looking young man in a hoodie had some sort of exchange with the woman with bright red hair before stumbling to the back seat and plonking himself down next to her. Frances was briefly distracted from her train of thought by her consciousness of his body odour and she shifted a bit away from him. Poor kid, he looked so miserable, she thought to herself. She became aware of an argument going on between the two women sitting at the front of the bus, and then the one with the red hair flounced off the bus at the next stop.

A few days after her precipitate exit, Frances had plucked up the courage to ring his parents once more to try to explain, but his mother had cut her short and hung up, leaving her even more tormented by guilt. Surely if she'd really loved him she would have stuck by him. But how could she have gone on when there was nothing left? His parents, especially his mother, had almost seemed to expect her, a young woman of 22, to take on being his carer even though they knew how new the relationship had been.

Frances had wrestled endlessly with all the possible scenarios, feeling that while she could never forgive herself for walking away, she could not have devoted herself to caring for Richard. Eventually she did talk to her friend Becky who had supported her decision without reservation, but she was still haunted by what much of her felt was treachery. One of the worst moments came when the Highways Department decided to make the turning into Longwall Street from the High Street a No Left Turn. Apparently another young cyclist had been killed there in very similar circumstances two years before, and another seriously injured only a couple of months earlier. Frances read about the proposed change in the *Oxford Times* and was enraged. Why on earth hadn't they done that before? If they had she might still have had the future she had been beginning to inhabit, and not the torrent of grief and guilt that had become her everyday.

She had tried to talk to her mother but got a predictable:

'I don't know what you're making such a fuss about – of course you can't be expected to look after him for the rest of his life.'

She hadn't really told her mother much about Richard – they had never been close. Her father had asked her about it, and he had encouraged her to talk about how they had met, what the relationship had been like.

They'd met over the photocopier at the language school where they both worked as teachers – her friend and flatmate Becky worked there too and had put in a good word for Frances when a vacancy came up. All three of them had gone for a drink after work. Richard and Frances had quickly become inseparable, sharing similar interests in music and movies, even football, and enjoying the same jokes. They'd been planning to move in together once Richard's lease on the flat he shared in the Botley Road ran out.

Frances had allowed herself to remember how happy they'd been, how fulfilling their sexual relationship and although they hadn't made specific plans beyond the next few months, how secure she'd felt about their future together. That six months had been idyllic, in a way that could never be relived. Even so, she wondered sometimes whether it had really been that wonderful, whether there had ever been rows or disagreements, whether she had ever felt let down or angry with him, or disappointed in him. She'd checked it out with Becky and her other friends who all said that they'd seen them as the perfect couple. Telling her wise and tolerant father about it had helped a bit. He hadn't said much but had seemed to gently understand and somehow that had enabled her to start to forgive herself.

Even so, seeing that spot again set off a wave of sadness and longing – and the ever present, blistering guilt. Perhaps she should have offered to care for what was left of Richard, perhaps that should have been the price to pay for the brief six months of happiness. How could she have abandoned him like that, and left his elderly, bewildered parents to cope? Did he go home to Manchester? Was he in residential care? She didn't know what had happened to him in the end or even whether he was still alive, fifteen years later. In the meantime she'd met Toby, dear Toby, who adored her and their children and who, in his quiet laid-back way, had helped her to gradually lay some of her demons to rest.

By now the bus was threading its way through the Northway estate and Frances was beginning to feel calmer. She jumped as her mobile phone rang. It was her mother, incoherent, tearful.

'Where ARE you? What's kept you?' Reassuring her mother that she was only minutes away, Frances felt the weight of dread. What would she find when her journey ended? The kind, cheerful, gentle father who had always made her feel loved and valued being apologetic for the trouble he was causing her, or another mute, frustrated, incapacitated wreck?

The hospital seemed familiar in some ways but there had been a lot of new building and the signage was more detailed but less consistent. As she drew nearer her destination the knot in her stomach seemed to tighten to an almost unbearable intensity, her heart was pounding and her armpits damp. She could feel the reluctance in her walk and the dread in her heart as she drew nearer the ward. Then she saw her father sitting up in bed and knew from his face that, at least this time, she wasn't going to have to go through all that again. 'Thanks for coming, old girl' he said. 'They say I'm fine.'

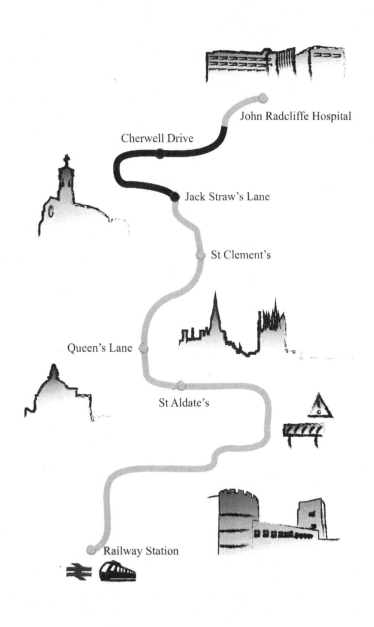

John Radcliffe Hospital

Cherwell Drive

Jack Straw's Lane

St Clement's

Queen's Lane

St Aldate's

Railway Station

Sweet Charity

JACKIE VICKERS

And now there was the business of clearing out Malcolm's things. Some friends had urged her to dispose of them, others said she should keep everything as it was, as if he had just popped out to the shops. Or, she could pack everything away. Joy herself favoured giving it all to charity, wouldn't Malcolm approve of that? In the end she delayed her decision and left all the golfing trophies, the golf clubs, car coat, even the two-seater sports car he kept for his own use, exactly where they had always been kept. She did put aside his mother's jewellery, as she had never liked his mother and the beads, as she liked to call them, were an irritating reminder of difficult afternoons when they had frequently been taken from their pig-skin case to be admired by a bored daughter-in-law. She remembered Roy Griffiths, a jeweller near the Marston shops, who had played golf with Malcolm. As her husband's old friend, he would surely give her a good price; he only opened Thursday afternoons, she might take it all to be valued. She could buy some new clothes, though Malcolm had left her more money than she could ever use. Still, there was something satisfying about selling his mother's brooches and necklaces to pay for the light-coloured silk shirts and dresses she had always desired.

'Not an inconvenient time, I hope?' The Reverend John Davidson patted her arm as he strode past and into her sitting room.

Joy made tea and cut a large slice of cherry cake.

'My goodness! You are spoiling me,' said the vicar, attacking his cake with enthusiasm. 'I don't know what Ruth would say. But then, we must be allowed to have some little secrets from our wives.'

Joy smiled. The only secrets that had come to light since Malcolm's death were a few extra charity donations.

'What can I do for you, Vicar?'

John Davidson was a tall, bulky man, and the chair creaked as he leant forward for more cake.

'This is just a social call. Making sure you are coming to terms with . . .' and he coughed.

Joy watched his large thick fingers curl round the delicate cup handle.

'You must miss Malcolm terribly,' continued the vicar. 'Such a good man. Believe me, it will get better in time.'

'My friends tell me I should keep busy with voluntary work, fund-raising perhaps. Malcolm did a tremendous amount, but he said my job was to "keep the home fires burning".'

'There's a place for all in every community. Malcolm was very good at fund-raising,' he added, 'and an excellent committee man.'

The Reverend Davidson stood up and moved to the window. 'Such a splendid garden,' he said. 'I imagine it kept Malcolm out of mischief.'

'Oh, no! Malcolm disliked gardening, he left all that to me.'

The vicar was still talking. 'It's a good size, facing south but with plenty of shade from the trees.' He half closed his eyes as if to see them better. The vicar rubbed his hands together and hesitated. 'But it may be too soon,' he muttered.

'Mrs Brightman is leaving us, and Hillside is up for sale. It has been such a splendid venue for our garden party, and as you know, the vicarage garden is such a small, sad affair. I was wondering how you felt about hosting it here?'

'Here?'

'It would give you an opportunity to show off your amazing, er, achievement. This garden needed a lot of work, as I remember.'

Joy closed her eyes and weighed the inconvenience against both the vicar's gratitude and the appreciation of the garden-party committee. 'I suppose there'd be help, with the tea and so on?'

'Oh, no end of help,' cried the vicar, sensing victory.

After he had left, Joy walked round her garden and breathed in the scents of early summer. 'Put in some trees,' Malcolm had said. 'This is your chance to plant your own copse, your own orchard. It's a rare opportunity to create a garden from scratch. Money no object.' It was nearly twenty years since they had moved some two hundred miles south of where they had both been born and brought up. It was a sudden move but was an opportunity not to be missed, Malcolm had said, not really explaining. Higher house prices had forced them into a smaller house, but one with a large, though somewhat neglected garden. Malcolm had been anxious to complete the deal and had emphasised the size and aspect.

'What sort of garden would you like?' Joy had asked.

'Do as you please,' he said, suddenly tired of the subject. 'There are vacancies on the Parish Council,' he told her, striding back to the house. 'I'll need something to occupy me while you're busy with all this.'

Returning indoors, Joy cleared up in the kitchen. Her day spread out before her with time for a little light pruning maybe and staking the delphiniums perhaps. She considered her half-empty fridge, satisfied not to see thick steaks and chops or the remains of a roast. At least she need not waste time food shopping. Her thoughts were interrupted by the doorbell. Joy removed her apron and glanced in the mirror before opening the door.

A girl stood on the step holding a small rucksack, which she put down in order to jam the door open. Joy saw scarlet, spiky hair, a studded face and cheap clothes. There was a long pause while they both stared at each other. Finally, the girl cleared her throat.

'I'm Malcolm's daughter. Can I come in?' She was out of breath and wiped her perspiring face on the sleeve of her jacket.

Joy looked up at the girl, unable to move, her heart pounding.

'That's a yes, then.' said the girl. She swung her bag over her shoulder and strolled into the sitting room.

Joy followed her. 'What do you want?'

'Tea would be good, two sugars, no milk.'

The girl was rude, uncouth, common, she thought, but that first look into those green eyes confirmed her story.

Joy put two mugs on the table, her hands shaking.

'You're wondering why I'm here.'

Joy said nothing.

'Malcolm Smith wrote to Linda, that's my mother: "please forgive me, I am dying", that sort of sentimental crap. It upset her, and do you wonder? Back when he heard she was pregnant he was off like greased lightning. Not one penny did she get off him. They all knew in the office, had a whip-round.'

Joy flinched at this and the girl raised her eyebrows. She turned away and wandered round the room, running her fingers along the back of the chairs, as if assessing their softness. She stopped to breathe in the scent of early roses in a bowl on the table, then, seeing Malcolm's photo, took it to the window where the morning sunlight glinted on the silver frame.

'Good-looking,' the girl said eventually.

Joy snatched the photo away and put it in a drawer.

The girl nodded. 'Quite a shock, I suppose.' She took a cigarette from her bag and lit it, breathing the smoke in deeply. 'Which is worse, then? Being Malcolm's deceived wife, living in comfort,' she waved her arm round the room. 'Or being his unwanted bastard child, living over the chip shop?' She sat down abruptly.

Joy watched the girl, sitting hunched over her cigarette, letting the ash lengthen and droop, her face tight with bitterness. Her short skirt exposed plump thighs and a hole in her black tights, her heavy black shoes scuffed the carpet. The girl crossed the room and put her mug down. Tall, big-boned, she towered over Joy. Despite her intimidating manner, she spoke well; her aggression seemed a veneer spread over a milder, gentler person. Nevertheless, she looked nothing like any child of Malcolm's she might have imagined; that child would have been small, slim and blonde.

'He never told you?'

Joy shook her head and shivered.

'Let's start again,' she said and closed the window.

The girl wanted to know everything about her father: which school he went to, his jobs, hobbies, his favourite music. Did he like Indian takeaways or posh dinners – she wanted to hear about everything Joy remembered.

And, because Joy sat mute, staring at her, she added: 'And then I'll go away and never come back. Couldn't afford to anyway. Have you any idea how much a bus ticket costs from Manchester?'

Joy sat still, as if paralyzed, watching, as the girl kept wandering around, picking things up. She stopped in front of a large framed photo, taken one Christmas, of Malcolm handing an over-sized cheque to a local charity for disadvantaged children. Volunteers crowded round with large toothy smiles. Malcolm looked very happy.

The girl prodded the picture. 'We could've done with some of that. Linda wouldn't have taken any money off him, not that he ever offered, but the odd tenner to me would've come in handy.'

'Well, it was up to your mother to ask,' Joy said, in a hard voice.

'I don't see it like that. I'm thinking of the moral responsibility one has towards others in society, let alone one's own family. I've just done three thousand words on that, so you could say it's uppermost in my mind?'

'You're a student?'

The girl nodded. 'Did Malcolm go to Uni?'

Joy shook her head. 'He couldn't afford to.'

The girl laughed. 'Neither can I.'

Joy glanced at the clock. If she didn't get rid of her soon she would be expected to provide food. She would want some lunch herself and the thought of preparing – then sharing – a meal with this person made her mouth run dry. Whatever the rights and wrongs, this girl was bright, determined and had travelled a long way, so she was not likely to leave without at least part of what she came for. I shall have to co-operate, Joy thought bitterly. None of this is of my making, but Malcolm had clearly seen what to do. Move on, live as though it had never happened. She would follow his example for the sooner she gave the girl what she wanted, the sooner life would get back to normal.

Joy stood up. 'We'll start with a simple family tree. Have you got a notebook? I'll give you some dates.'

But there was a lot more to Malcolm's life than could be crammed into the hour before lunch.

Tired now, Joy was irritated. 'Why didn't you ask Malcolm about all this?'

'I didn't know his name or where he lived until I saw the letter he wrote. He's not even on my birth certificate.'

Joy made sandwiches, tea and still the girl wanted to know more. Eventually she asked for a keepsake, so Joy had selected his school tie and golf club membership card, as neither meant much to her.

On the whole the visit went well enough, after the first shock, though there had been a difficult moment when the girl had looked through the pile of charity leaflets. She had pointed to an aid worker cradling an emaciated African infant.

'Posh school, good education, I'll bet. Never missed a meal in her life. Poverty, what does she know?'

And Joy wondered what Malcolm's daughter knew of life. Drugs perhaps, abusive boyfriends, abortions, who knew what else.

'Some say charity begins at home.' The girl twisted her mouth in a bitter smile. 'A difficult one, that.'

Joy went into the bedroom to hunt out some early photos but when she returned to the sitting room, the girl had gone. The note said: *Got what I came for. Carly.*

The smell of smoke and cheap perfume had lingered and Joy opened all the windows. The girl had not asked for money. 'She could see she would get nowhere with me!' Joy said to herself with satisfaction, taking Malcolm's photo out of the drawer and replacing it by the golf trophies.

It was Thursday again. Already a week had passed since Carly's visit. Joy had tried hard not to think about the girl, it was too disturbing. It all happened twenty years ago, another time, another place. That Linda was probably asking for it and followed him around, no doubt, hoping to ensnare an older man. All men get tempted, she thought, clearly Linda should have behaved better. And what an outrageous thing for Carly to do. She should have had the good manners to stay out of Malcolm's life, not hound him beyond the grave with her unlikely story of wanting to know her father. Joy had spent the time since Carly's visit in the garden. Fresh air and exercise took her mind off the girl and her awful mother. She understood now the urgency that lay behind their sudden move, glad that it had given them twenty peaceful years, giving Malcolm the freedom to devote so much time to the charities he supported. 'Our small contribution to improving society,' he would say, always including her, never taking all the credit. But now she felt tired and needed something else to occupy her in the remaining few weeks before the garden-party. She was not yet ready to allocate Malcolm's personal possessions, but the small pigskin case and its contents was something easily dealt with. And Roy's little shop opened on Thursdays.

The car tyre had a puncture. For a moment Joy suspected Carly, even though the car was in the garage, for she had never had a puncture in many decades of driving, surely too much of a co-incidence. Then she saw the nail. Her own carelessness when sweeping up. She hesitated. A short walk down Jack Straw's Lane would take her to the bus-stop. On the other hand, she never travelled by bus and was it wise, taking such valuable items on public transport? But then she would surely not be robbed in broad daylight on a bus in Oxford, and afterwards she could call at the nearby garage and get someone to mend her tyre.

A crowd of students, Chinese maybe or Korean, she didn't know the difference, boarded the bus ahead of her. She sat at the front holding her bag close. No-one would think of taking anything from someone sitting so near to the driver. There was the added advantage of not having to look at the other passengers, an unprepossessing collection from what she observed every time one of them boarded the bus. The journey seemed to take no time at all and Joy wondered, briefly, if she should not take the bus now and again and save on parking. She got out at the Marston parade of shops and walked round to Roy's house, where he did business from a small room with a large safe.

Joy opened the pig-skin case and took out various necklaces, bracelets, ear-rings and an unusual brooch. Roy leant forward with an eager smile, pushing everything aside, except for the brooch. 'The emerald is a good one,' he said, peering at the stone through his lens, 'and the setting is very well done, twenty-two carat, fine filigree work, nicely proportioned. A rather exceptional Art Nouveau piece, much sought after. I could give you a good price – you say it belonged to Malcolm's mother?' He put his lens down and started to fidget with the silver chain. 'Are you sure, Joy? Are there no family members who might like it?'

Joy frowned. Clearly this brooch was far too valuable to be passed on to a girl with scarlet hair and studs. She would only sell it.

'I shall be giving the proceeds to charity, as Malcolm had no female relatives,' she said, closing the pig-skin case with a loud click.

John Radcliffe Hospital

Cherwell Drive

Jack Straw's Lane

St Clement's

Queen's Lane

St Aldate's

Railway Station

Unlucky 13?

JENNY BURRAGE

Triskaidekaphobia (from Greek tris meaning '3', kai meaning 'and', deka meaning '10' and phobos meaning 'fear' or 'morbid fear') is fear of the number 13 and avoidance to use it.
(Wikipedia)

The name Bramwell Bentley was in many people's opinions a very superior name. His mother, Helen, had thought so and his father had complied with his wife's decision to choose that name before his son was born. It was unfortunate that Bramwell was born on Friday the 13th August 1965 because his mother was superstitious, some would say obsessively so.

She held her newly born at arm's length for some time.

'He's an unlucky baby, you see,' she explained to one and all. 'A Friday-the-13th-baby, very bad news.'

Her husband was not remotely superstitious and declined to comment. He guessed she would come round eventually, which of course she did. Indeed she loved her baby son but his date of birth and its consequences remained uppermost in her mind. Yes, Bramwell Bentley was doomed to be unlucky in life. She was determined that this would never be, not if she had anything to do with it. She would be a powerful force to be reckoned with. It was fortunate that baby Bramwell was taken home to Horseshoe Cottage. A horseshoe hung above the front door, its ends pointing upwards to collect any good luck that happened to be floating by.

He turned out to be an only child and that put Helen Bentley's entire motherly focus on her son. He would need special training and continuing guidance throughout life so that he would always be lucky. His star sign was Leo, meaning he would be a strong leader and the old nursery rhyme said that Friday's child was 'loving and giving'. That was the good news, but his date of birth, the 13th, seemed to overshadow everything.

One of his first memories involved shoes. Young Bramwell once had the temerity to put his new trainers, worn in the rain, on the kitchen table and examine them for mud.

'Get those off the table at once.'

He jumped. His mother's voice was so loud.

'Why, Mum?'

'Because it's unlucky.'

He was to hear those words so often as he grew up.

After the ticking off, the phone rang with a message to say he couldn't go round to have tea with his friend George because George had forgotten he was having an extra piano lesson that very evening.

'I told you,' said Mother. 'That was bad luck, Bramwell.'

His mother was always right or so she informed him. His father seemed to think she was always right because she had told him so as well. The two males didn't stand a chance to think for themselves.

The training programme for Bramwell probably all escalated with the ladder incident. When Bramwell was about seven, he and his mother went shopping at M&S in Oxford to buy him a new school uniform. As they approached the store, a man was cleaning the windows of the adjacent shop. Bramwell had stopped holding his Mother's hand and skipped round under the ladder to greet her with a beaming smile at the automatic opening door. The surrounding shoppers were amazed to hear the shouting.

'Now you've done it. You've really done it this time, you naughty boy. Don't you remember what I told you about ladders?'

Bramwell had no idea what she was talking about so she told him again that it was very unlucky to walk under ladders. Bramwell decided he would tell the next window cleaner who came to their house about the dangers. As far as he could see, nothing bad happened afterwards except that the new school term started next day and that meant the end of the summer holidays. He'd enjoyed the holidays. He supposed that was the bad luck.

The mirror episode was another one of the other times he remembered well. It was perhaps the most horrific. The family had just had a new bathroom installed but something was missing, a mirror.

'It's totally incomplete,' his Mother told Bramwell, 'without a mirror. I shall borrow one from the visitor's room until your father can fix a new one up.' Bramwell couldn't see what all the fuss was about because he never looked in mirrors anyway. He went downstairs but heard a crash and a scream almost immediately. Rushing back up he found his mother on the floor and the mirror in a thousand pieces scattered around the room.

'Seven years bad luck.' She was screaming and moaning alternately. She had slipped on the newly tiled floor. Bramwell stared. What should he do? He went next door for help. Neighbour Sally was in.

'Stand well back, Bramwell,' she said when they went upstairs. 'When I have made your mother a cup of tea, I shall clear up the mess. Fragments of glass can be dangerous.' Bramwell was pleased to see his mother upright once again. It had been very scary seeing her like that but she was still on about the bad luck.

'Seven years,' she said to Sally, tears falling into her mug of tea.

'Rubbish', said Sally.

When Bramwell had his thirteenth birthday, his mother was dreading the day. She made plans.

'We shall call it your un-birthday,' she informed him. 'We shall refer to it as your baker's dozen celebration.' Bramwell thought that was a splendid idea. He liked the thought of buying a dozen cakes and getting an extra one popped in the bag for luck by a kindly baker. He loved his mother's amazingly clever ideas. It was unfortunate that both sets of grandparents sent birthday cards showing the number thirteen. So did his school friends. Helen did not want to throw them away so she got to work with the Tipp-Ex and some felt tip pens. Now the cards had a new message for Bramwell which read 'Happy Birthday 12+1.' Bramwell's friend stared at the graffiti.

'Who did that?' he asked.

'I did,' said Helen. 'Thirteen is so unlucky, George.' When

he thought about this, George wasn't really surprised. It was typical of Bramwell's mother. When his father saw the cards, he smiled secretly. Madness he thought, but he kept very quiet. Better that way.

Of course Bramwell's life hadn't been totally about bad luck. Oh no, there was good luck too. He and his Mother spent hours in the field at the bottom of the garden searching for four leaf clovers. When they did find one, there were cheers all round and Helen showed him how to press the clover inside a book so you could preserve it.

Bramwell was also surprised one early Christmas, when he was five years old, to find a furry object in his stocking when he woke up that morning.

'It's a rabbit's foot,' his mother told him. 'It is very lucky.' Bramwell didn't think it was lucky at all. He felt sorry for the rabbit. He hid it away.

And then there were the rhymes that she was always quoting like,

> *See a pin*
> *Pick it up*
> *And all day long you'll have good luck.*

There was a rhyme about counting magpies which puzzled him,

> *One for sorrow,*
> *Two for joy,*
> *Three for a girl,*
> *Four for a boy,*
> *Five for silver,*
> *Six for gold,*
> *Seven for a secret,*
> *Never to be told.*

Bramwell wondered what the secret might be. Secrets were like puzzles and he loved solving puzzles. He'd seen a picture of a magpie in his bird book but he'd never seen one in real life.

His grandparents (on his father's side) were concerned about him and his upbringing. They thought him a very impressionable boy and they were not too keen on their daughter-in-law, Helen.

'All that nonsense about bad luck, poor boy,' said his grandmother. 'It's not good for him. He's a very bright lad. She's brainwashing him.'

It was really no surprise when Helen joined a local Feng Shui group, as she said, in order to bring peace and harmony to the home. According to the ancient Chinese rules, one could organise one's home to promote an energy flow in every room. Accordingly, certain colours were essential for walls, furniture must be positioned carefully and specially patterned rugs purchased. The house was certainly different. Both husband and son rather liked the changes and it kept Helen happy.

When Bramwell eventually left school and went to Magdalen College, to read modern history, he didn't leave home. Why would he when he lived in Oxford? Helen was delighted. She could continue keeping tracks on his wellbeing, carefully monitoring his chance for good luck and keeping the bad luck at bay.

The supervision increased when Bramwell began having girlfriends.

'I would like to meet her,' said his mother every time a new relationship developed. It was extremely important that her son's chosen partner should be an Aquarian, for, according to astrology, Leo and Aquarius star signs were matched in harmony. Unfortunately each girl was subjected to a battery of questions. They also discovered that Bramwell's mother was such an important part of his life, they felt shut out.

'Your mother's weird,' said one girl but Bramwell didn't think so. He was used to his mother's ways. She was protecting him after all.

So here he was at fifty years old, unmarried, with a first class degree, and still living with his mother and father at Horseshoe Cottage. The Friday-the-13th-baby had survived thus far. His father, now retired and in his seventies, seemed perfectly happy to tolerate his wife's obsession. After all he had his golf now.

Bramwell still automatically followed certain superstitions.

For example he always said 'White Rabbits' on the first day of every month and never ever opened his wet umbrella to dry inside the house. As for salt, if he spilled any, he naturally always tossed some over his shoulder for luck. He never walked under ladders either. Not any more. Habits he had never shaken off.

The number 13 was different. It had been a constant shadow in his life. Today there was a problem because on his way to the JR hospital, he had to catch bus number 13. He shivered. 13. The epitome of bad luck. He was always aware of this number, unlike his automatic responses to the other superstitions. Whatever would his mother think if she knew he was about to visit her by travelling to the JR on a number 13 bus? She might have a second heart attack.

Pity he'd never learned to drive. He could always take a taxi. Don't be ridiculous, he told himself. You know the number 13 is an ordinary cardinal number used in daily lives. All the same he felt apprehensive. 13. Unlucky 13. He closed his eyes but the numbers were still there in his mind. Large and black. Looming.

He walked from his office in Hythe Bridge Street to the train station and waited at the bus stop outside. Almost instantly it drew alongside, the bright orange number 13 staring blatantly at him, as if daring him to board. He got on quickly and paid, his hands shaking, choosing the first available seat somewhere in the middle. There was a woman in a smart suit making a commotion at the front of the bus. He looked away. The sooner his journey was over the better.

At one point the bus lurched forward. Accident he thought, this is it, but it was just the driver being careful and skilful in avoiding an unaware pedestrian. After that, nothing. He was soon off the bus, somewhat relieved, and heading to the hospital.

Once inside, just as he stared at a board to find directions to the correct ward, he saw a rather buxom woman in nurse's uniform coming towards him.

'Bramwell,' she said. 'Bramwell Bentley. I can't believe it. It can't be.'

He searched her face for a moment and then he knew.

'Linda. This is amazing. Haven't seen you since school.'

'You don't look much different, Bramwell. I remember you as the brainiest boy in our class.'

He laughed. 'How are you doing, Linda?' He'd always liked her, remembered her as good fun. Even as a schoolboy he'd fancied her. He'd never had a long-term girlfriend. Mother made sure of that. He wondered if she was married. Couldn't see a ring.

'I'm fine thanks. Nursing in the cardiac unit.'

Bramwell was amazed. 'What a coincidence. That's where I'm going. To visit my mother. A heart attack, they think. Last night. It was all very sudden. My father's visiting this evening.'

Linda thought for a moment. 'Of course. Helen Bentley. I didn't realise she was your mother. Didn't make a connection. I'm on a different ward but I've seen her briefly.'

Something happened to Bramwell as he looked at Linda. A mind flash. His mother was no longer around. At the moment. He was free.

'Look I know you haven't got time to chat now but maybe we could meet up. I would love to see you again, Linda. I'm planning to move into a flat.' Yes. That was his next move. He decided on it in that instant. He should have done it years ago. The 13 bus had brought him luck and he was going to make the most of finding Linda.

'You OK Bramwell?' He realised he'd been deep in thought.

'Sorry. Just thinking about us meeting like this.'

She smiled. 'It would be great to see each other again when we've both got more time. I'll give you my card and you can text me. Or phone.' She took one out of her handbag. 'I'll most likely finish my shift about six or seven and should be home by eight if you want to catch me this evening. You could even come for supper. I live on my own now. I'm sure I can rustle something up. In any case, you may see me around the unit when you are visiting your mother. Come on. I'll show you where she is. I guess she'll be there for a while longer.'

'Touch wood', said Bramwell.

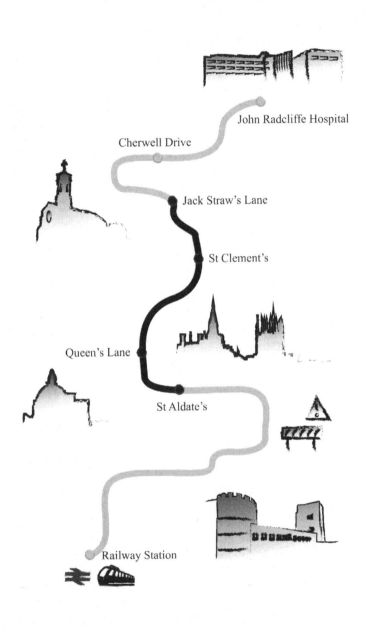

The Best is yet to be . . .

JACKIE VICKERS

'Do I have to?' Ellie looked down and glared at her mother. She was sitting at the top of the stairs wearing an outfit which her mother suspected had been taken from the community recycling bin.

'I'm not leaving you behind, not after last time.' Kate stood by the door, rummaging through her bag for her keys. 'Get your things, I don't want to be late.'

Kate regularly drove to Oxford to visit her mother Betty, who had moved to *The Willows* after Christmas. Ellie had no objection to visiting her grandmother. She did object, however, to sitting in a metal box with her mother for the hour it took to drive there and the further hour to drive back. Ellie had pleaded a headache before the last trip, then called her friends. They took advantage, Kate had complained, but Ellie argued she was only following instructions to be more sociable.

'But having friends round does not mean cigarettes, cider and possibly under-age sex.'

'I wish!' said Ellie, rolling her eyes.

Moving into *The Willows* had been Betty's idea. She had visited a good many homes with friends of hers, who were also trying to find the best answer to the problem of ageing and failing health. They made light of their excursions, for as Betty reminded their little party:

'If we take this too seriously we might get really depressed, so, laugh away girls!'

Eventually she made her decision, found a solicitor and paid a deposit. Then she told Kate.

'But you'll lose your independence. And all your memories are bound up in your house.'

'There'll be help when I need it, all meals provided and no washing or cleaning. And, I shall no longer be alone. As for memories,' Betty tapped her head, 'my memories are in there.'

So Kate had conceded, much to Betty's amusement, that perhaps her mother knew best and she and Ellie accustomed themselves to visiting *The Willows* alternate Saturdays.

The Willows was a substantial late Edwardian house, which had been built for a local businessman and his large family. When his descendants found the house and grounds too extensive for their needs and too expensive to run, they were sold to a national organisation running some fifty care homes all over the country. During the latest recession it had been decided not to economise on personal care, food or heating. Inevitably, cuts were made on maintenance.

'It could all do with a lick of paint,' Kate told her mother, picking at a peeling window frame with her thumb-nail. 'There are stains on the carpets, and a great gouge in the plaster in the hall. It gives such a bad impression.'

They were sitting in the garden on a warm March afternoon. Betty allowed the sun to warm her face for a while before explaining.

'Accidents happen more often when you get old. Arthur gets dizzy and spills food; Dorothy is still learning to steer her new wheelchair.'

'But you used to keep your house pristine, doesn't this neglect bother you?'

'Perhaps I did too much cleaning. It's just so unimportant in the grand scheme of things.' Betty pointed her stick at a clump of late crocuses. 'It's better to spend time enjoying the flowers.'

Precious secured the velcro straps on Betty's slippers and straightened up, gasping.

'You get more puffed than I do,' said Betty.

This was not surprising as Precious had eight ladies to 'assist' every morning. 'Assistance with personal care when required' headed *The Willows'* mission statement. This glossy brochure had a picture of a smiling elderly couple below a slogan in bright blue letters: 'facing the future with dignity'. All Precious' ladies required assistance and none of them liked it, though some were more polite than others. Betty was one of the nicer ones, except on the days when her daughter visited, when she became difficult and insisted on walking without her frame.

'Is young Ellie coming today?' Precious liked to see the grandchildren visiting. They wore their best clothes and came clutching teddies or play-stations to see them through the boredom while her ladies and gentlemen confided their troubles to middle-aged children, or, more often, fell asleep. Ellie was one of the older ones, plugging music into their ears, sitting apart, tapping their feet.

'My daughter complains about Ellie. But she was much more trouble at that age.' Betty threw her head back, laughed and shuffled off towards the day-room, one hand clutching the rail. Dorothy was waiting at the usual table, gazing out of the window while Arthur fussed with packs of cards.

'Kate's coming today,' Betty announced as she lowered herself slowly onto a chair. 'But there's time for a few games. Ah, here comes Leslie.'

A tall, thin man walked briskly up and emptied the contents of a plastic bag onto the table, so that chocolate bars, toffees and boiled sweets rolled about. Arthur, who had been told he was pre-diabetic, hastily hid his share. They glanced guiltily around, but the staff were all busy and the four card-players settled down to their regular morning game.

Ellie sat in the passenger seat, eyes closed, feet tapping, fingers clicking.

'I want to talk about Gran.'

'What?' yelled Ellie.

Kate pulled the wire out of her daughter's ear and the car swerved. The car behind honked and she clenched her hands on the wheel. She saw the lights change, but was flustered and stalled the engine.

'I can't wait to pass my test,' said Ellie, putting her ear-piece back.

'I want to talk now. You can listen to this any time,' shouted Kate, grabbing at the wire again. 'What do you think about having Gran to live with us? Now that your father isn't coming back we have the room and it will be better for Gran to have a proper home.' Kate waited, but Ellie said nothing.

'Well, what do you think?'

'Why ask me? You seem to have decided.'

Kate took deep, slow breaths and counted up to ten. 'I need you behind me on this.'

'Why?'

'I might need some help now and again.' There was another long silence, then Ellie sighed.

'I think it's a rubbish idea,' she said, picking at her nails.

'Aren't you being a bit selfish?'

Ellie shrugged. 'What is Gran going to do all day when you're at work? I don't get back till four and in a couple of years I'll have left home.'

'She might make friends.'

'She's got friends now.'

'Well, I get upset about her being in that awful place.'

'So this is all about you then?' Ellie gave Kate a triumphant look and pushed her earpiece back in.

When the tea-trolley came round, Kate slipped away to look for Precious, who was sitting in the care-workers rest-room with her feet up on a stool. She looked up from her magazine.

'I don't want to disturb you, but how is my mother?'

Precious blinked. 'Betty is over eighty.'

'But her health, it hasn't deteriorated unduly, recently?'

Precious looked at her own swollen feet, felt the aching in her joints, thought of her blood-pressure tablets.

'We are all deterioratin',' she said, turning back to her magazine.

'There are no significant changes then.'

'Significant,' repeated Precious.

Kate tried again. 'Is she happy here?'

'Has she told you she isn't?'

Kate sat on the edge of a chair and leant forward. 'You see, I should like to offer my mother a home with me, as my personal circumstances now make this possible. But I need to be sure there are no underlying health problems, physical or,' she hesitated, 'mental.'

Precious sighed and put her magazine down. 'Have you asked her what *she* wants?'

'Of course not. I don't want to get her hopes up. Suppose you were to tell me – I don't know,' she looked up at the ceiling for inspiration, 'let's say her sight was failing, she might not cope with my being out at work all day.'

A few days later, Kate collected her mother for a trial week at home, though she told Betty it would be a little holiday. Easter was late this year and Kate's garden was full of spring flowers. French windows opened onto a paved area dotted with tubs of daffodils.

'It's the perfect place to nod off in the sunshine,' said Betty on Easter Sunday.

But Kate had made plans. 'We can do that any time. I thought you might like a trip to Hillside Manor. It's only open four days a year and it would be a shame to miss it.'

Kate knew that the elderly are often left out of family excursions, and was determined her mother should get out and see things. She expected Hillside Manor would be an ideal venue, for there was disabled access and even wheelchairs for hire. It took a long time to get Betty ready, and the roads were congested with Bank holiday traffic, so they arrived late. Kate's arms soon ached from pushing the wheelchair up so many slopes and it was difficult to hear what her mother was telling her. She needed to sit down.

'The tea-room looks nice and there isn't too much of a queue.'

Betty nodded enthusiastically. She had a stiff neck from craning up to see the pictures. Everything was too high for her, it was like being a child again.

'Just park me at a table then you'll have your hands free.'

'But you'll want to choose your cake.'

There had been a run on Betty's favourites and the only choice was between walnut, which got between her teeth, and lemon drizzle which gave her indigestion.

'It's the Easter Quiz today,' Betty told her daughter, when they were settled. 'We were favourites to win.'

'Who's we?'

'Our team. Arthur, Leslie, Dorothy and me, only Leslie's in

a dream most of the time.' Betty removed a walnut from her cake.

'What was the prize?'

'A big box of chocolates. I wonder if they'll think to save one for me.'

'I thought you were supposed to avoid chocolate.'

Betty smiled, thinking of Leslie's trips to the shop.

Towards the end of the week Kate got a call to go in to work. Ellie was back at school, so who would look after mother? Kate was worried about being late, she still had to help her mother dress and sort out her lunch and iron her top.

Ellie picked up her schoolbag and gave her mother a look of contempt. 'Who will look after Gran if she comes to live here?'

'I'll get a support system underway.'

'You mean you'll ask the neighbours.'

'There are people in every community who like to help out, to feel useful.'

'Why should Gran want help from total strangers? They may be your friends and neighbours, but they're not hers.' Ellie strode out of the house, slamming the door behind her.

The house was very quiet when Kate had gone out and the time passed slowly. By eleven, Betty decided to relieve the boredom by having some lunch. Kate had left a tin of soup out, but Betty had little strength in her hands and could not open it nor could she manage the bread knife, for there was no sliced bread. The old lady rooted around in the well-stocked fridge, but found only food she could not digest, or that was not to her taste. She then tried the tins for cake, biscuits or something comforting, but found only rice-cakes and wrinkled her nose at the smell.

'All this healthy food, no surprise she's always tired.' She squinted up at the calendar. 'Thursday, It's plum crumble.' She sighed, 'I'm missing the plum crumble.'

Ellie flew in at four and put the kettle on. 'Surprise!' she shouted, waving two chocolate bars. She carried in a tray with two mugs of cocoa, a pack of cards, a handful of coins, and the chocolate. She showed Betty the coins.

'We can play for higher stakes today!'

When Kate came home she complained the room reeked of chocolate.

'There's plenty of fresh fruit around. It would be healthier for both of you.'

She had noticed that her mother appeared to have eaten no lunch. Food was proving a problem as none of the evening meals she suggested suited Betty, who could not digest anything spicy or rich. Later that evening Kate leafed through cookery books.

Ellie rolled her eyes, 'Why don't you just ask Gran what she eats at *The Willows*?'

Precious straightened up with a sigh and started on the cardigan. 'Have a good holiday?' she asked, slowly moving Betty's arm into the sleeve.

Betty nodded.

'Did your daughter mention her plans?'

'She's always got plans. I don't always listen.'

'About you going to live with her?'

Betty swayed slightly. She looked around and thought of the familiar faces waiting for her in the day-room and her eyes filled with tears.

'She can't make me leave, can she?'

Precious shrugged. 'Jus' telling you what Kate's thinking.'

A few days later Precious called Kate at work. 'Nothing to worry about,' she said, 'but your mother was complaining you never visit.'

Kate was anxious and drove over after work. Betty was cheerful, glad to see her and they spent a pleasant hour together. But the next day Betty complained to Precious again.

'Everyone else has visitors,' she said in an aggrieved tone.

That weekend Kate insisted that she and Ellie should spend time discussing these developments.

'How do you know Precious wasn't making this up?'

Kate poured herself a large whisky. 'What if this were the beginning of dementia?' she said, ignoring Ellie's question, 'what then?'

'The sooner she moves in the better, you can always give up work to look after her if she gets really bad.' Ellie gave a mischievous smile.

Kate filled up her glass. 'Don't be ridiculous. If I leave work, I'll never get back to the level I'm at now.'

Ellie shrugged. 'Do you want to know what I think?'

Kate drained her glass. 'I'm not sure that I do.'

'I really liked having Gran here for that week. But she would go off her head living here.'

Kate sat back and closed her eyes. 'Ellie, they do their best at *The Willows*, but the carpets are stained and they smell. Then there's another smell at meal times, usually boiled cabbage. The place is so shabby, and the toilets are not as clean as they should be. My mother was a fantastic cook and a fastidious housekeeper and I can't bear to see her in that place. At least here I have Elena coming to clean twice a week.'

Ellie stood up and faced her mother. 'Old people don't need clean carpets and gourmet food, they need to be somewhere they can be happy. Gran likes to be with people so she would hate it here, on her own all day. All our neighbours are at work or at school.'

'She would make friends eventually,' sniffed Kate.

'Why don't you ask her what *she* wants?' Ellie began to pace up and down. 'What is so difficult about talking to her?'

'You think it's easy for mothers and daughters to communicate?' Kate asked, filling her glass again.

'Not when one of them is full of whisky.' Ellie grabbed Kate's glass and poured the contents over a pot plant.

'Killing that cactus won't help.'

It was now late June and, with Ellie's exams well out of the way, Kate suggested a shopping trip. She had noticed her daughter was less argumentative, easier to be with and as a gesture of reconciliation said they might find clothes which were acceptable to both of them. Their outing was going well when Kate was interrupted by a call from Precious.

'I don't want to worry you, but your mother has taken to callin' me Lily. An' gets angry if I try to correct her.'

'It'll take forever if we go back to the Park and Ride, with this traffic. We'll take the 13 bus, there's a stop fairly near. We can get off at Jack Straw's Lane and walk through.'

They hurried along Cornmarket, dodging the crowds and reached the stop as the bus drew up. Ellie moved aside as a passenger helped his much younger companion down the step. She watched as the woman stumbled on the uneven pavement, almost falling into the man's arms.

Kate prodded Ellie. 'Get on!'

They sat down on the first empty seats, struggling with their carrier bags.

'It would have been easier in the car,' said Ellie, pulling a couple of Kate's bags onto her knees.

'I told you. There isn't time.'

A crowd of students, laughing and elbowing each other tried to get on at Jack Straw's Lane but were held back by an older woman, the driver showing considerable patience as she fumbled over her fare.

Kate started to run.

'Slow down Mum! Gran's only confused, it's hardly an emergency. Wait for me.' But Kate did not slow down, nor did she wait for Ellie.

Betty suggested a walk in the garden, which meant a slow shuffle towards the nearest bench. The old lady became animated by the show of spring flowers.

'I do like dahlias,' she said, sitting down with a contented smile. Kate tucked a rug round her and said she thought they might be tulips.

Betty nodded, 'I get muddled sometimes. They've got such good gardeners here. Do you know, they mow the grass before breakfast. What do you think of that?'

Kate could not think of anything to say, so she patted her mother's hand.

Betty turned and grabbed her arm. 'Karen, you did remember the marmalade?'

Ellie saw the distress on her mother's face. 'Why don't you have a word with Precious while I sit here with Gran.'

Kate rushed erratically back towards the house, stumbling over non-existent obstacles.

Betty turned to Ellie. 'I haven't overdone it have I?'

Ellie grinned and pulled a couple of chocolate bars out of her pocket. 'You can always make a miraculous recovery, once the dust settles.'

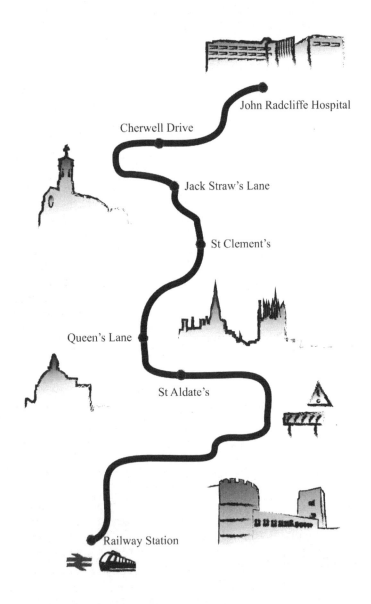

On the Buses

ANDREW BAX

It was nearly 50 years before Keith realised his childhood ambition. Like most young boys he wanted to drive a train, a bus or a fire engine. But when he left school all he could drive was his motorbike and he was well into his twenties before he got his first car. Most of his working life had been spent doing dead-end jobs – warehouse work mainly. Then he was made redundant and thought he was heading for the scrap-heap. Who, these days, would take on an unskilled 56-year old? It was on the way to sign up at the Jobcentre that he saw the notice in the bus: 'Drivers wanted – training provided.'

That was six months ago and it changed his life. After an interview with the Oxford Bus Company and a medical test by his GP, he joined an intensive training programme. Within days, it seemed, he was reversing double-deckers into spaces with only six inches to spare on either side. After all this time he discovered he was a natural. When he had completed 40 hours with an instructor on the road and passed a one-hour driving test, he got his Passenger Carrying Vehicle Licence. There were hazard-perception tests and then an examination on theory. Health and safety, driving hours, regulations – stuff like that. Keith had never taken an exam before and was full of gloom. But he was determined; he studied the books and DVDs diligently and, to his great relief, he beat the 85% minimum pass mark.

That wasn't the end of it though. He then had to earn his Certificate of Professional Competence which covered practical aspects of the job such as evacuation procedures in the event of fire, dealing with troublesome passengers and what to do if he was involved in an accident. Finally, it was route-learning, including the location of hundreds of bus-stops. After three weeks, Keith was exhausted, elated and a fully-qualified bus-driver.

There was something majestic about driving those big, red

Scanias through Oxford's crowded streets but, when the novelty had worn off, he had to admit they had their downsides. Their suspension was quite hard, gusts of wind caught their sides unexpectedly and a fully-laden double-decker affected the steering. On top of all that you had to keep a watch-out for low branches and shop awnings. Now he preferred the single-decker Mercedes Citaro, which is what he was driving today, on the JR run.

Swinging into the station forecourt, Keith reflected that his redundancy was the best thing that had happened to him. At the stop he lowered the platform to pavement level and opened the doors. The bus emptied itself of passengers and a few more got on, including a little old Chinese-looking lady, wearing a backpack nearly as big as herself. She asked him how to get to All Souls College; Keith didn't know but another passenger said she would tell her where to get off.

He was just about to close the doors when one of the station staff hurried up to the bus, carrying a case for a smartly-dressed woman, tottering behind him on high heels. 'I need to get to the John Radcliffe Hospital as a matter of urgency', she announced loud enough for the whole bus to hear. Keith indicated the taxi queue but she wasn't finished. 'And I want you to take me,' she said, and sat down. The man gave him a £20 note, winked and got off, but she showed no interest in taking her change. With a shrug, he decided to put it into the collection box for the Oxford Radcliffe Hospitals Charitable Funds.

He didn't like the money side to the job; with passengers hurrying to get on, asking him for directions and giving him notes when he didn't have much change, it was easy to make a mistake. If the takings were short at the end of the week they were deducted from his wages.

Keith eased the bus into Frideswide Square, along New Road and into Castle Street. There he joined the line of buses waiting at the lights controlling access to St Ebbe's. On green they began to thread their way through the wasteland of construction sites that would, one day, become Oxford's new shopping destination. Nine minutes behind schedule, his No 13 arrived at the first major stop of the journey,

St Aldate's. There was always a queue to get on there and he nodded a greeting to some of the regulars. When they were loaded Keith closed the doors and, pulling into the traffic, cut a swathe through the crowds ambling across Carfax, and turned into High Street.

Among those waiting at the Queen's Lane stop was Neil, ready to take over the bus so that he could have his tea break. Keith crossed to the ticket office and, as he was deciding whether to have a Belgian bun or some lardy cake, or perhaps both, he asked if anyone knew where All Souls College was. Just across the road, they told him, 50 yards up on the left. So the Chinese-looking lady should have got off at Queen's Lane. Keith wondered if she did; he didn't remember seeing her.

Neil had been a driver for decades and had seen all the changes. Sometimes he would regale his colleagues about life as it was when he first started. Saturday nights – you took your life in your hands! There was no fun driving on your own with a bus-load of drunks for company. Sometimes, of course, they were after the money and the only way to get help was to look for a payphone, if you could find one that was working. Now it was all CCTV and radio contact. Drivers even had a spit kit in their bags, the same as used by the police, so that offenders could be traced through their DNA. No-one had used it in years but when Neil first started it was not unknown for agitated passengers to spit at the driver. Things had certainly changed for the better. They even had women drivers now.

After a year or two, Neil lost his first enthusiasm for driving. It was the same routine every day: same kind of buses, same kind of routes, same kind of passengers. Like many people in his position he found relief from the sameness of his work in a hobby, in his case, model railways. Currently he was building a 4200 tank engine in 00 gauge, and he was a perfectionist. Not for him the kits made from pre-formed plastic. He worked from the original plans, cutting the components from metal sheet, rod and block and, when he had finished, the wheels and pistons would move just as they should. He started work on the engine three years ago and reckoned it would take at least another eighteen months to complete. Most nights, when he was not on the buses, he would be in his workshop using watchmaker's tools and eyeglass and a tiny lathe, to replicate in faithful detail the version which first saw service in 1910. As a child Neil was forever taking things apart and putting them together again. He could have been an engineer, his mother said, or a surgeon. Instead he was a bus driver.

He glanced in the mirror at his passengers. Apart from two women shouting at each other it was the usual lot of stuffed dummies, most of them engrossed in electronic gadgets. They must lead very boring lives, he decided and he was certain none of them had the excitement of creating such a master-piece as his 4200 in its full GWR livery.

Just then a young woman, mobile phone clamped to her ear, put one foot on the platform while still standing with the other on the pavement. She was blocking others trying to get on and reacted angrily when one of them tried to get past her. Then, with a cry and her face suddenly paled, she pushed her way back onto the pavement. Waves of irritation passed through the bus. Neil muttered to himself; if there was one thing that really annoyed him it was people talking on their mobile phones while buying a ticket. It was just plain rude.

He started the bus and headed down High Street. At the lights cyclists swarmed out of Long Wall Street without looking, and swept along the inside as he approached the Plain. Neil sighed; you saw some crazy driving while on the buses, and cyclists were probably the worst. Weaving all over the road, turning off without signalling, riding after dark without lights. They were asking for trouble, and some of them didn't even wear helmets.

Then, as they approached the bottleneck of St Clement's, an elderly woman stepped into the road, causing the traffic to brake sharply. She was at the pedestrian crossing but she didn't wait for vehicles to slow down for her. Neil had seen quite a few near-misses there. It was the wrong place for a crossing because the road was so narrow at that point, hemmed in by buildings on either side, and you couldn't easily see pedes-trians when it was busy.

The incident unsettled him and he was in no mood to sympathise with a scruffy young man who got on at Marston without enough money for his fare. He wanted to go to the hospital, a ten-minute walk away, and Neil had to control his exasperation. However, one of the other passengers paid the difference, and they moved on.

By the time the No 13 pulled into its final stop at the John Radcliffe it was seven minutes behind schedule so he had to load up quickly and make the return journey back to the station. Only then did he notice a little old Chinese-looking lady still sitting there, still waiting for someone to tell her when to get off for All Souls College.